Love Letter to Lola

PRAISE FOR
LOVE LETTER TO LOLA

Carmel Bird is an extraordinary writer, and these stories are playful, violent, wild. In *Love Letter to Lola*, she asks us to inhabit the bodies and minds of birds and insects, mammals and angels as they—as we all—stand tremulous on the point of extinction. Reading them made me feel braver. – **Sophie Cunningham**

Playing with darkness—but in no way mucking around—this teeming collection is deeply tuned to the possibilities of a future 'where all life on the planet is treasured and nurtured by humans'. – **Gregory Day**

A beguiling blend of historical facts – with an eye for the unexpected and bizarre – and a dazzling imagination. A vividly realised world of fantasy, romance, and horror, in which animals voice the brutal realities of species extinction and the destructive effects of colonialism. There's profound emotion and disarming wit, with faint echoes of optimism about the future of the planet under siege. Vintage Carmel Bird: immersive, surprising, and irresistible. – **Susan Midalia**

These stories are in love with life and its surprising possibilities. They are clever, heartfelt, joyous, and wise. They find, as Hopkins said, the 'dearest freshness deep down things.' Time spent with Carmel Bird is simply uplifting. – **Michael McGirr**

Once again Carmel Bird weaves her magic, constantly surprising the reader with her inventiveness and her wisdom. Reading her stories is like opening up a compendium in which one finds unexpected treasures. Hers is a unique voice, attuned to the disquiets of our age and still able to inspire hope and reflection.

– Dennis Altman

With *Love Letter to Lola,* Carmel Bird can rightfully take her place as one of the finest short story writers in Australian literary history. On the back of an already stunning body of work, this collection – rich, unnerving, playful, terrifying, and heartbreakingly moving – pushes the limits of the genre to such a satisfying and effortless degree that you feel you are reading something entirely fresh and new. Bird's stories teem with life, they eddy and dance, and flow back and forth through each other, like memories and history and life. They may be told from the perspective of a cockroach, or a mournful brother, or an angel, and each and every one of these stories is thrillingly convincing. As a writer, Bird has been and continues to be impossible to categorise. Her ideas and obsessions and interests are multitude, but all without exception are driven by her utterly unique, pyrotechnic energy. Her stories roar and soar, they set your teeth on edge and trigger tears, they make you howl with laughter even as you peer into the abyss of existence. This is the thing about masters of their craft – they reignite in you the unquantifiable joy of reading. And if they're good enough, they also make you excited about the complex art of writing. How on earth, you ask, did she just do that? Carmel Bird is one such master.

– Matthew Condon

ALSO BY CARMEL BIRD

Telltale
Field of Poppies
Family Skeleton
Child of the Twilight
Cape Grimm
Red Shoes
The White Garden
The Bluebird Café
Cherry Ripe
Unholy Writ
Open For Inspection
Crisis
The Dead Aviatrix
The Essential Bird
The Common Rat
Automatic Teller
The Woodpecker Toy Fact
Births Deaths and
Marriages

Fair Game
Dimitra
The Mouth
Dear Writer Revisited
Not Now Jack –
I'm Writing a Novel
Writing the Story of Your
Life
The Stolen Children –
Their Stories
Red Hot Notes
Relations –
Australian Short Stories
Daughters and Fathers
Home Truth
The Penguin Century of
Australian Stories
The Cassowary's Quiz
Fabulous Finola Fox

LOVE LETTER TO LOLA

CARMEL BIRD

SPINELESS WONDERS
PO Box 220
Strawberry Hills
NSW Australia 2012

shortaustralianstories.com.au

First published by Spineless Wonders 2023

Published by Bronwyn Mehan

Typeset in Garamond Pro
Image source Shutterstock
Printed and bound by Ingram Spark
Distributed by NewSouth Books through Alliance Distribution Services

ISBN (pbk) 978-1-925052-96-1

A catalogue record for this book is available from the National Library of Australia

Who can tell
Where the comedy
Cuts out
And the tragedy
Sets in
– **Carrillo Mean** *The Moan of Doves in Moama*

There was never a Queen like Balkis,
From here to the wide world's end;
But Balkis talked to a butterfly
As you would talk to a friend.
– **Rudyard Kipling** *Just So Stories*

The well of inspiration is a hole that leads down
– **Margaret Atwood** *Negotiating With the Dead*

When the Titanic sank, we thought it was a miracle
– **The Lobsters** *In the Kitchen*

For Edith and Sebastian

CONTENTS

Animals

Humans and Angels

ANIMALS

LOVE LETTER TO LOLA

A letter from Spixi, a blue macaw, member of the *Cyanopsitta spixii* family.

Melância Creek, Bahia, Brazil
Christmas Eve 2000

Lola, My Lovely,

Forgive me for writing this letter on the reverse of a fragment of the Basurto dinner party invitation. Alas, this is all I have to hand. I know you will understand, my darling. Here in the back lands of the disappearing green fringes of the caatinga forests, paper is scarce. I write with bright pink juice from the cadaver of a goat, knowing the colour will please you. My instrument is a spine from a fat old cactus. Today, in memory of you, I have feasted well on the seeds and juices of your favourite faveleira. My thoughts have been filled, as they forever are, with pictures and sounds of you, my dearest Lola, my childhood sweetheart, my own.

My rational mind tells me you have gone, have gone; yet in my heart of heart I hold you still, beloved, and I know you will hear my love song as I write to you, you in your resting place in the great beyond.

I recall the joyful days when, together as one, we steered our course, our long blue tails flexed against the air, through the tip tops of the caatinga. I recall how we would come to rest, almost floating into the ancient family home. There in the nest chamber you tended our three rare and precious unhatched chicklings. Deep inside the hollow of our tree.

Then, there flashes upon me the memory of the dark edge of doom. In the eerie light before the dawn, the drone of the vehicle. The trappers. We huddle together. The trappers whisper as they scratch and scrape at the walls of our house. The gloved hand—then the arm enters, feeling for you, for me, for the eggs. Like fine thin glass the pure white shells are shattered. The yolks, blood-streaked, flow and drip into the bottom of the nest. You clamber up, heading for the exit, the circle of faint light as the radiance of the pre-dawn leads you on toward freedom. I follow. You spread your darling wings. You enter the net that awaits you.

In the horror of panic, with my heart pounding, there was nought for me to do but struggle past. Forgive me, forgive me, my own, for I could not save you, although I saved myself. I flew in blind desperation into the trees, away.

All this happened exactly thirteen years ago on Christmas Eve, 1987, my blue bird of eternal happiness and sorrow. I write this letter to tell you of my love for you, and also to set down the sad and complicated story of our lives. As daylight came and you lay in your dreadful cage in terror, a cheerful and curious stranger approached the trappers on foot. They showed him their prize, my lovely, my Lola, and with his Polaroid camera he took a picture. There it was, gradually forming on the paper, an image—pale grey head, great black beak, sharp yellow eyes, brilliant turquoise dress feathers, and your long, long blue tail—it was you. The last wild girl ever, captured and sold into the slavery of the zoos. It was three years before the scientists, seeking our kind in the wild, saw this picture and realised they were looking at you, the last, my last, wild girl. They played their tape recordings of our call, played our music to your Polaroid, my love.

I was alone in the forest. I searched for you, I flew on and on and I sought you, I sought you down the nights and down the days, down the years and years in baking sunshine and when rain fell upon the earth. I could never have imagined such loneliness, such sorrow, such despair. You were the last wild girl, I the last wild boy.

Those scientists who came to the forest in 1990, they sighted me, the lone bird, in the early daylight, and they gazed at me through their binoculars, and they filmed me with their video cameras. I called for you, and they recorded my sad call. *Kraa, kraa, kraa.* Should they capture me, they wondered? Should they? It took them two more years to decide they would leave me in the wild. But they had interesting plans. A miracle was about to occur.

After my seven sorrowful years of solitude of being apart from you, my rarest, my most beautiful, my most coveted Lola, in 1995, suddenly, among the dappled light and shade of the waxy caraiba leaves, *you were there*. Not the dancing hallucination of my dreams, but the long-lost shimmering, gleaming turquoise princess of my days. They had released you, given you back to me.

Unable to believe what had occurred, we flew in an ecstatic and bewildered trance, feasting not only on the faveleira trees, but also on delicious pinhão and juicy joazeiro. The short three months we were together remain the strangest, the brightest, and ultimately the saddest months of my life. This time you were not stolen, my lovely Lola. You flew, my dearest, by accident, into the invisible new electric power lines, and were killed.

I can scarcely believe the bitter cruelty of fate. I mourn for you for all eternity.

I must confess to you, my own, that my lasting faithfulness to you has, over the years, been spoiled yet not dimmed. For in my loneliness, I have sometimes had the companionship of our cousin, Linda, the little green Maracana. I knew her slightly during my seven years of isolation, and yes, she sometimes joined us on our journeys in 1995. Forgive me. You do not wish to know the rest of the story. We flew together, Linda and I, in the daylight, and usually I took her back to her own family at night. I slept alone on the top of a prickly cactus. And I defended our old home from the many others who wished to colonise it. In 1996, the year after I saw you, my lovely, for the last time, Linda and I moved in together, and there were three eggs, but even they were stolen. In 1999 the scientists brought for us some eggs from my cousins in a zoo. With great joy we hatched them, and they flew with us. I do not know where those children are now. Naturally, I fear for them, knowing what I know. Linda and I have now parted company.

It is thirteen years, or five thousand days and nights, since first you were stolen away from me, only to return for those three brief months of joyful life. On this Christmas Eve, the first of the new century, I am secretly at large, undetected by the scientists and the trappers. I fly on in lonely longing, writing this letter to you on the sad anniversary of the time when first I lost you.

I shall but love thee better after death,
Your ever devoted
Spixi

A response to the letter, from one of Spixi's distant cousins, a certain Primo, a member of the *Primolius maracana* family.

Maracana Blue Wing School of the Air
Brazil

To Whom it May Concern

Unlike Linda in Spixi's story, members of my family are blue, not green.

In 2022, I discovered this tragic, heartbreaking note, long, long after it was written. I assume Spixi himself has died, and those young ones he mentioned flew off to their doom. The letter was caught on the thorns of a desert cactus, crinkled, and fading and crumbling. Such poetry!

I believe this letter is in fact a key document behind the scientific experiment I am taking part in. And I can tell you that whenever I ponder Spixi's letter to his beloved, I am inspired all over again to play my part. Spix's macaw has been known as 'Extinct-in-the-Wild' since poor old Spixi disappeared. But there were still a few of them in human captivity. The important thing was to get them going out in the free fresh air.

Impossible? Turns out it's possible. And I am proud to be part of the solution.

The thing was that the scientists needed to work out how to get the poor old Spixes to go back and live in the wild. So, they got hold of some captive-bred ones and, in June 2022, they released four pairs of these into the caatinga. Exciting! And every one of them was wearing a GPS tracking gizmo. Modern life at its navigational best, you might say.

Now the scientists, thinking all the time, had captured a number of my wild people, including me, and they took us by aircraft out of Brazil and off to Germany. Imagine. In a German lab they trained us for our task, then brought us back here to Brazil. They said we had to get around with the captive-bred Spixes and teach them how to survive out here in the wild.

That's how the Maracana Blue Wing School of the Air came into being. We have to tutor the Spixes on how to forage, what to eat, how to get water, how to communicate, and how to recognise and avoid the big old predators. Funny really, about the predators, because the worst one is the human being, and yet it's human beings who are organising the experiment. It takes all sorts. I've got my own GPS, of course. All the Spixes have to go back to the Release Centre every night. Then they come out in the morning, and we help them to get on with it in the caatinga. Do this, do that, go here, go there, look, listen, fly for your life.

I'm used to it now, but it's quite a different existence from what I thought I was going to have. If I sometimes get a bit tired of all this mentoring, I only have to read through Spixi's letter to Lola, and I realise I am part of a Great Plan, and I let out a joyful ragged squawk that rips right through the desert air. I call it the Sound of the Spirit of Optimism.

(*Signed*) Primo

MARGARET ORB-WEAVER, THE INTERVIEW
19 SEPTEMBER 2022

Note: During the television coverage of the funeral of Queen Elizabeth II, many viewers were able to detect, crawling across the white card among the flowers on the coffin, a small green spider.

My little sister Margaret is gone forever now. She has fulfilled her destiny, or if you will, her task in life, and we may never see her like again. With the eyes of the whole world upon her, she gave her final interview, which I reproduce here. I believe there is no better way to tell her story, and no finer way to immortalise her. We are incredibly proud of her, and while our hearts are heavy, our souls will always sing her praise. Forever and forever.

(Signed) Lily Orb-Weaver, on the leaves of the second rosemary bush from the end.

The Interviewer: I understand that as a member of the Orb-Weaver family, you are here on this historic day to perform a sacred duty.

Yes, we were first invited way back in 1547 to watch over the royal Orb whenever it accompanies the dead body of the Sovereign to rest.

Do you do Coronations?

They don't need us at Coronations because in that case the Orb doesn't travel around. But the final journey is one of particular significance, when the Orb—and the Sceptre of course—are left behind at the end, and the body must go on, as it were, alone.

What happened in 1547?

That was the funeral of the eighth Henry. In fact, he had a much plainer Orb. The Lord Protector, Oliver Cromwell, later had it melted down. The one you see today was made for the first Charles when he was crowned in 1661. The archbishop still says the same words when he places the Orb in the hand of the Sovereign. 'Receive this orb set under the cross and remember the whole world is subject to the Power and Empire of Christ our Redeemer.' Or words to that effect. Very grand. I've never actually heard him say it. Never had the chance to witness a Coronation. Well, there hasn't been one for what, seventy years or something.

Could you give the viewers a quick description of today's Orb?

With pleasure. It's a rather heavy hollow golden ball representing the harmonious whole of the universe. A strangely bored, yet meticulous, ancestor of mine at one of the funerals counted the number of pearls on it—three hundred and seventy-five—ten more than the number of diamonds. He sent a message home giving all the statistics. Yes, three hundred and sixty-five diamonds.

That's quite a lot! A diamond a day.

I should think so. And eighteen rubies and nine sapphires.

I believe there is an amethyst.

Amethyst, yes, my favourite. And a piece of glass.

A piece of glass?

Yes, glass was quite a thing in 1661. And it's just a reminder.

Of what, exactly?

That not everything can be pearls and diamonds and so forth. It's actually a lovely piece of glass, I can assure you. Make no mistake.

Oh, quite. And there's a handsome cross on top of the Orb, I notice.

Yes, that really sets the whole thing off, to my way of thinking. You realise the ball itself is a reminder of Jupiter. You know, the Roman sky god.

A Roman god. How so?

Well, Jupiter was the top god of the Roman pantheon. Having the Orb is a link to that whole ancient thing. The Christians naturally added the cross—it's more or less their signature, isn't it? The whole Coronation business means the Sovereign is appointed by God. Amazing idea, really. How would that work, I wonder.

And you were saying the tradition is for the green Orb-Weavers to accompany the Orb at the funeral when the coffin is displayed in public.

It is. We do. I am the next in line for today's specific task. A distant ancestor last did the work back in 1952. It's a suicide mission.

Why a suicide mission?

After the Lord Chamberlain breaks his magic wand over the coffin, showing that this particular carnival is over, I am to remain with the flowers and leaves when the coffin goes down into the vault. The Orb, with the Sceptre of course, will be safe above ground but, having performed my duty, I will be with the body of the Sovereign. I look forward to hearing the muffled mournful notes of the lone piper as we descend into the abyss.

I see.

Once down there I might spin a last web among the rosemary. A last trap, a last insect, a last supper. But basically, I'm out. Dust to dust you know. As I said, it's a good seventy years since an Orb-Weaver enjoyed the privilege of all this. I'm pretty lucky really.

I suppose you are. And I believe that today you were able to read what was written on the card that was resting among the flowers.

It was very sweet. It just said: 'In loving and devoted memory—Charles R.'

I probably don't need to tell you that today you have become quite the celebrity yourself.

How is that?

You were photographed climbing along the card, and your picture has been all over the internet. Social media. News.

Oh, how interesting. The family will no doubt be pleased. But of course, you realise one of our distant relatives has been incredibly famous for over two thousand years.

Er, I am not actually aware …

She was in Bethlehem that time when King Herod ordered the soldiers to slaughter all the boy babies. She hurried down to the stable and wove a curtain right across the doorway, so when the soldiers came looking for the Baby Jesus, they thought the place was derelict and deserted, and they just moved on and killed some other babies. It was a huge job, doing the web. That was partly why we were given our shape and chosen to guard the Orb. In recognition of our role in the Bethlehem event.

That explains a lot!

Oh, I thought everybody knew all that.

Many of the old stories have been lost. But thanks to your gracious granting of this interview, now everybody knows. You have brought us the news from over the centuries.

I have heard there is quite large body of fake news these days. Webs of lies and so forth. It must be difficult for you, working in the media. Something I did learn today—you see those big black furry helmets on the heads of the Grenadiers?

I do. What did you hear about them?

Apparently, according to my sister Lily's boyfriend, they have to slaughter a hundred bears from Canada every year so they can keep up the supply. And that's the truth. Rather cruel, whichever way you look at it.

I see. Well, everyone can be certain that all you have told us here today is the truth, simple and unadorned.

I can swear to that. And now the procession is moving on, and I must say my last farewell. Sic transit gloria mundi.

And so, Margaret Orb-Weaver moves slowly into history, into eternity, as she proceeds, concealed within the delicate green petals of a hydrangea from the Palace. Thank you, and farewell.

RESURRECTING MARTHA

Once upon a time in America there lived a man (A) whose job it was to examine the dead bodies of creatures such as birds. It's a long time ago now, 1914 in fact, and one day in a laboratory in the great museum in Washington, the man performed a necropsy on a very special bird, while another man (B) took photographs of the procedure. Skeleton and organs and flesh and skin. The dead bird was the last member of the species *Ectopistes migratorius*, commonly known as the passenger, or the wanderer pigeon. She was twenty-nine years old, and had died of sadness and old age, a captive in the zoo at Cincinnati, five hundred miles from the great museum in Washington.

It was just over a month since the murder of an Austro-Hungarian Archduke had caused the eruption of the Great War.

The corpse of the wanderer had travelled from Cincinnati by rail, frozen in a huge block of ice, which, during the three-day journey, was reduced to a puddle so that the wanderer arrived at her destination as a bedraggled little bunch of bones and feathers. She was transformed into a statue of herself by a process of taxidermy, and was put on display, a silent sorrowful figure, marked as being extinct. Her breast was cinnamon rose, her iridescent throat and neck feathered lightest bronze, pale mystic green, soft shadowy purple. Brownish grey, her head and back. Bright red eyes, small black bill. Feet and legs were a gleaming crimson lake. Her name was Martha.

Artists have immortalised Martha in paint, alongside her late husband whose name was George and whose hues were brighter than those of Martha. They were named for Martha and George Washington. Rich wild copper, viridian, Tyrian purple. George died in the zoo in 1910 but nobody thought to send him off by train to Washington on ice. He was tossed down a convenient well. Like George and Martha Washington, the pair of wanderers had produced no offspring. Disappointed visitors to the zoo liked to spatter the lone and mournful Martha with handfuls of sand, hoping the little captive widow huddled in the cage might hop or dance or run or fly or sing. Or at least spit? Red eyes, black bill, iridescent soundless throat. Red shoes.

Back in once upon a time in 1900, a woman (C), who preserved another wanderer, the last one in the American wild (the bird had been shot by a teenage boy), ran out of red glass eyes with which to decorate her specimen. The woman searched and searched in vain for those elusive red glass eyes, and then she gave the female bird, instead, a pair of shiny black shoe buttons. Because of her distinctive little eyes, the last *wild* wanderer came to be known as Buttons. She is on view at the Ohio Historical Society in Columbus. Her colours resemble Martha's, a reflection of the glittering sunlight that shimmers high, high in the heavens above the roof of the Ohio Historical Society in Columbus.

The flocks of wanderers had once been enormous beyond imagination, the areas of land they occupied when nesting, likewise. The numbers recorded are so large they are magical—or meaningless.

One of the artists (D) who have rendered Martha and George in exquisite glowing detail also wrote an account of a gigantic flock of wanderers along the Ohio River that blotted out the sun for three days as they streamed, steadily, like a mighty river across the sky. One naturalist (E) is believed to have observed 3,717,120,000 wanderers passing overhead in Fort Mississauga, Ontario. The largest nesting of wanderers occupied 1,162,751 square kilometres and destroyed forests with the weight of the bodies of the birds.

Magical or meaningless.

They had the devastating power of a great tornado. Their music was soft, a kind of chattering and rushing that rose from the vast woods as if the trees were sighing. Oak trees were stripped of their acorns, crops in the path of the flock were reduced to empty ravaged fields of useless, dying stubble. The favourite dessert foods for the invaders were ripe red strawberries and rich red cherries.

Once upon a time in America, well fed, the wanderers provided a swirling, glinting, flying economical bright-feathered dinner plate for the humans. Giant nets were constructed for their capture. Guns loaded, too. Or take a stick, reach up, stun your pigeon, and take him home for supper. Once upon a time.

It was a short length of time, forty or so years, and in that time the numbers went down from maybe five billion creatures in the 1870s to the forlorn one of Martha, in 1914, showered with sand in her cage in the Cincinnati Zoo. Is all this real or is it imaginary?

In 1565, the first Europeans began joyfully eating the wanderers, until that day when there were no more wanderers to eat. Smothered Pigeon was a popular dish: Dredge four pigeons in flour, salt, and pepper. Brown them in butter. Add onions, carrots, and celery. Pour in stock, cover, cook in medium oven for one hour. Garnish with chopped parsley. Benedictus, Benedicat. Gleaming fat. Suck the juicy meat from the spindly bones. Toss the bones into the black iron cauldron of the stock pot for another day.

Later on, somebody invented the telegraph, and then somebody constructed the railway, and news travelled, and wanderers in enormous quantities were quickly transported into markets all over the country. *Passengers are requested to make their way to the barrier.* Smothered Pigeon and Pigeon Pie and Mrs O'Malley's Pigeon and Potato Puffs. Soon there were more dead wanderers than live wanderers, moving about in great heaps in rattling railway cars and landing on a million billion menus far and far and wider than wide. Grilled Pigeon with Prickly Pear, Chile, and Tequila. For what we are about to receive.

Then—nothing.

Passengers are requested to make their way to the barrier. The party is over, and the fat of the bodies of Z-billion flying pigeons has been translated into fuel for the bodies of Z-billion humans, and there is chilly joy and hollow laughter. Time passes. Times change. God used to make the wanderers, but all that is over now. He who wants to sup on the dreamy cuisine of Mrs O'Malley from down in the valley will need to tiptoe to the laboratory where the Folk of Science are cooking up the latest thing in pigeon. Is this a good idea, or a bad idea? It's an idea.

Remember Martha and the cage in Cincinnati? Well, on a public wall in downtown Cincinnati, Martha and her whole flock are represented in a large and vivid painting by (F). There she is, so pretty, leading the pack across the heavens. Go Martha! She alights in Sausalito, California, where, in a bright and shining laboratory, the Folk of Science, like the alchemists of long ago, are on the job. They work with the deoxyribonucleic acid of a wanderer, *Ectopistes migratorius*, who does not exist, and with the deoxyribonucleic acid of a band-tailed pigeon, *Patagioenas fasciata*, who does. The Folk of Science aim to edit the two sets of genes and manufacture a brand-new wanderer, a resurrected Martha, a brand-new George, with the devastating power of a great tornado. Genius! For what we are about to receive. Rich wild copper, viridian, Tyrian purple.

Imagine the skies above America where giant aircraft criss and cross among the clouds, transporting living human bodies hither and thither every minute of every day. *Passengers are requested to make their way to the barrier*. On the tiny tray-tables sit neat packets of delectable Pigeon and Potato Puffs. Mrs O'Malley would be proud. Some of the low-lying clouds are composed of new wanderers blotting out the sun. Catastrophe and Deja-vu. An item on the evening news.

It sometimes looks as if the humans are taking over the job that once belonged to the gods. A wise man (G) once said that if this is the case, then the humans need to 'get good at it.' Maybe the Folk of Science in Sausalito are getting good.

As a matter of fact, for millions of years humans have worked at reproducing birds—and trees and animals and so forth. Art, it's called art.

Imagine a peace-filled garden, within castle garden walls that shelter trees, flowers, a spring, four women, two men, one baby, an angel, a tiny dragon, and a small demon, far from the dangers of a violent world. There is food on the table and, on the walls and in the trees, there are birds. The woman (H) in the centre is reading a book, the baby is playing a psaltery. That swift flight of imagination is a description of a work of art, a painting, *The Little Garden of Paradise*, done long ago early in the fifteenth century by the artist (I). The lone wanderer, or something very like her, sits on the top of the cherry tree, feasting on favourite gleaming crimson food, delighting in the harmony of illustrated life.

The painting lives in peace in the Stadel Museum in Frankfurt. But peace does not last forever.

One fine day, along comes A with his sharp, sharp instruments, one of the Fabulous Folk of Science and Art. The cleverness of them! He places the little painted garden scene, so safe, so sweet, on his slab at the museum in Cincinnati, and he digs and scrapes away at the wanderer posing cheerfully on the cherry tree. Flicks the body onto flat clean cold surface of the slab. Click goes the clever camera held by the trusty B who records in his magic manner the crop full of cherry stone, the quietly whispering feathers, the fragile skeleton revealed and laid out upon the slab. Globe of skull with beak and eye-socket. Ribs. Long plaited rope of spine forming a delicate arc across the surface of the slab. Bones of the wings, splayed out on the cold hard surface. Click goes B, documenting everything, everything final and dead and gone. Dead and gone. Mutilated cherry tree where no bird sings. The baby plays his psaltery, the woman reads her book. The demon lurks in shadow beside a budding tree stump.

Ectopistes migratorius, adieu. Hasta la vista.

List of Characters

   A   William Palmer
   B   R. W. Schufeldt
   C   Mrs Barnes, wife of Sheriff C. Barnes of Pike County, Ohio
   D   John James Audubon
   E   William Ross King
   F   John A Ruthven
   G   Stewart Brand
   H   Virgin Mary
   I   Unknown Upper Rhenish Master

THE COMEBACK AND THE POND OF DREAMS

'Hope' is the Thing with Feathers
Emily Dickinson

All this has been a very long time coming. I wish I could speak to you from the future, a time when I will exist again in the corporeal medium. Meanwhile, consider me as the Spirit of the Species. While I am replete with hope that the attempts to manifest me will be truly successful, I acknowledge there can be no certainty in these matters. My existence is in the hands of the deities, the magicians, the technicians, the scienticians, and probably a few other categories of specialists. These beings are all devoted, diligent and, in many cases, gifted with the light of what I might call genius. However, as you will realise, I am a difficult case. They say it is proving harder to resurrect me than it is to bring back the *Thylacinus cynocephalus*. I love the scientific names for things, my own being *Raphus cucullatus*. I am much better known as Dodo. I am a creature of mystery. I am an enigma. This fact may be a great part of my charm and fascination. And then there's the matter of my non-existence. Some people have chosen to believe I have *never* existed. That too is a cause for fascination. What price the unicorn? I make an appearance on the coat of arms of Mauritius, me on the left and a sambar deer on the right. The deer are not yet extinct but give them time. Somebody called Johann Van Der Puf designed this in 1906. His name has a certain ring to it, I suppose. Does it make me immortal? Maybe? Or what.

One of the most important specialists in worldwide research into me/us is Dr Kenneth Rijsdijk at the University of Amsterdam. You can find Ken online at his site called *Dodo Alive*, which is a pretty good and optimistic name, you would agree. He and his colleagues investigate the DNA of dodo bones. Imagine! It was the Dutch, by the way, who set the Extinction Machine in motion in my case.

Long, long ago, Arab and Portuguese sailors visited my island. Then, towards the end of the sixteenth century, Dutch expeditions were out and about on the briny deep, a glint in their nautical eye, seeking trade throughout the East Indies. In 1598, C.E. Dutch ships visited the island, and reports in 1601 spoke of the dodo. The sailors generally didn't like us as meat, except for our stomachs and breasts. Apparently. They preferred eating the coo-coo turtle doves, which seems reasonable. In our stomachs they found the stones we used/use to help us digest our own food. I remember the stones. Most subsequent reports mention the difficulty people had in cooking and eating us. No problem catching us, no problem at all. And all kinds of artists simply loved to draw and paint dodos—not always from life. And they still do. The Spirit of the Species and the Image of the Species—everywhere you look. There are many, many copies of copies of copies. The truth will out when the Comeback is complete.

By 1690 there were no dodos left alive on planet Earth. Sad Face.

It might be a bit of a race between me and Thyla the thylacine for the Comeback, but we will both get there, or should I say here, in the end—or the beginning. Breathless Excitement! There is something timeless about the times I am discussing, so you will have to forgive me if I appear to go back and forth, or round and round in weaving, wandering circles. When I say 'I' you must understand this first-person pronoun refers, as I have said, to the Spirit of the Species. And if you look at a map of the world you will see Thyla and I used to be (are) separated geographically by more or less open sea. There was Thyla, sometimes known as the Tasmanian stripy tiger, roaming around Van Diemen's Land looking for prey while I was happily marching about like some cheerful swan on Mauritius, gleefully swallowing quantities of fruits, seeds, nuts, bulbs, and roots. And generally mixing with flamingos, giant tortoises, lizards, parrots, and suchlike. It was a pretty sight. I had no predators. (Cue human beings.) Of course, Thyla lasted longer than I did, back then, but fizzled out in the Hobart Zoo in 1936. (Read on for more news of Thyla.)

I imagine you might have first encountered the idea of me in the work of Lewis Carroll, who even identified himself with me, and who showcased me as a character in his great book of 1865 C.E. He used to visit my tragic remains (a foot, a head, mummified) in the Museum of Sciences in Oxford, and these vestiges stirred his imagination, as why wouldn't they. Accompanying these sorry scraps of the physical life of the species was a portrait of me painted in 1626 by Roelant Savery, a Dutch master of the still-life. You would almost certainly recognise his glorious bowls of flowers with their sprinklings of lovely little zippy lizards and insects. (Forgive me, won't you, if I get carried away with the adjectives.) His picture of me was the inspiration for the later interpretation by Sir John Tenniel. It was the

Tenniel image, illustrating the story by Lewis Carroll, that rocketed me to a kind of fame, and placed me as the poster-bird for the Extinction Industry. I beat Thyla to that by quite a long way, didn't I? Thyla became the go-to extinct mammal towards the end of the twentieth century and, in a great flurry of scientifical excitement, they decided to make an attempt at bringing us poor old creatures back to face the twenty-first century music. Cue crashing cymbals and groaning organs.

I will be needing gendered pronouns in a minute, and I confess I don't know whether the Spirit of Thyla is male or female, but I can tell you I was/am (trouble with tenses again here) female—a fact I imagine is useful to the work of the scientificators, should they truly want to crank up a new branch on my family tree. How can a spirit have a gender? Search me. Of course, it may be possible, after the first Comeback of the species, for that Comeback to be cloned, and for the clone then to undergo a change of gender. I am sorry, but I don't have all the answers, and I must trust in the skills and imaginations of the deities and magicians I mentioned earlier. They once did some funny work with sheep, and also with the ears of mice. They're mighty clever, you know. For one thing, they grow human beings in glass dishes, I believe. I hear that one swallow does not make a summer. That makes sense, doesn't it. One new dodo will be thrilling, but two will be necessary if dodos are to make the full glorious Comeback to rollicking racy vitality. No glass dishes for us! Of course, I am nothing like a swallow, no streamlined darting bluebird of happiness, me. I should say I am the antithesis of a swallow. After a good deal of scientical discussion and argument, it was decided I am/was a giant flightless bird of the pigeon or dove kind, a sort of earth-bound waddling Holy Ghost. I'm a little bit afraid I might end up as a Comebackatoo or somesuch. That reminds me to tell you that dodos murmur like well-mannered pigeons. Really sweet and low and comforting.

In my corporeal manifestation I am thirty inches tall, and I weigh about fifty pounds. My head and bill are enormous, my wings minute, and my tail feathers truly splendid and nicely curly. I am very proud of my tail feathers, by the way. You can tell. My legs are short, my claws large, scaly, and powerful. My colours are a lovely grey, mingled with some yellow and green. So, you see, nothing like a swallow. If you must know, the colours are somewhat nondescript, or, you might say, subtle. I walk in an upright fashion, and I possibly resemble a swan. Yes? Early on the whole island was *called* Swan. But it's not that they are going to write a ballet called *Dodo Lake* any time soon. Or isn't it? As you will see, this idea is not completely out of the question. For one thing, people are turning into robots as we speak. Read on.

Hope, as the great Emily Dickinson said, is the thing with feathers.

You will be wondering how the foot and the head ended up on display in Oxford. I will explain. In the early seventeenth century, an Englishman called John Tradescant the Elder collected a vast number of strange and rare objects from near and far. He opened the first public museum in England, the Musaeum Tradescantianum. Two of the rare objects were, you guessed it, the dodo head and foot, which later were displayed in Oxford, and exposed to the gaze and imagination of Lewis Carroll, who advertised me to the world as the creature that said, 'Everybody has won, and all must have prizes.' I don't believe I ever really said that, but I might have. Perhaps I have forgotten. It's been a while. It doesn't really sound like me, though.

You will also be wondering about where I came from, and when and how I faded out to the point where all you have are weird old scraps and the Spirit of the Species. Well, to tell you the truth, these days there are bones—they have found bones—even a full skeleton. However, I believe a Comeback requires a bit of soft tissue. But more of that later. For now, think distant exploration, think sailors, think cats, rats, pigs, and monkeys. Invasive species, yes, that's what *they* were. Destroying the habitat and eating the eggs and scaring us out of our feathers. Are you sitting comfortably?

So, think long ago, think eight million years ago. Think Africa. Think ocean. Think volcano. And vroooom-whoosh-kaboom! Great disturbance of the waters. Then, there you have the island, twelve hundred miles off the south-east coast of Africa, in the Indian Ocean. My island home. Today you will know it, since 1992, as the Republic of Mauritius, famous for its beaches, lagoons, reefs, and sunsets.

In the sixteenth century, the Dutch ships came and, long before the sun had set on the seventeenth century, *Raphus cucullatus* had been removed from the island forever, removed from the face of the very earth itself. Extinct. Last seen, in fact, in 1662 CE. In the nineteenth century, a few bits and pieces remained to be marvelled at, and also subjected to a certain amount of searching scientifical research.

But now I bring you to the Pond of Dreams. You have been most patient. And here's a great new term for you: subfossil material. The story is hotting up! So is the planet, of course, hence bringing me and Thyla back from our extinctions might be just a luxurious and eccentric exercise of dancing in the darkest, darkest gloom-dark dark that follows the End of the End.

The Pond of Dreams is a natural storage facility in which are found the preserved bones (and sometimes even soft tissue) of animals, including dodos, in an anoxic medium where bacterial activity is minimal. I enjoy my borrowings from the scientificators. This is your subfossil material, as promised. The pond is more of a swamp than a pond, really, and is located close to the sea on the south-east coast of the lovely island of Mauritius. In 1865 (the same year John Tenniel's picture of a dodo was published in Lewis Carroll's book—cue coincidence) after searching for thirty years among the dreams of the pond, a Mauritian schoolmaster named George Clark finally found, in the deepest part of the water, the preserved bones of dodos. (Quiet and meditative notes on a silver flute.) Collection of our bones from these waters has continued, and examples are now found in museums all over the world. The only known complete skeleton was assembled by Louis Etienne Thirioux, a quiet and somewhat mysterious Mauritian barber, yes, barber, who died in 1917. Quite recent, in the scheme of things. The Scheme of Things—I love that phrase. Do you suppose there might be a Scheme? This skeleton is kept in the Natural History Museum in Port Louis, Mauritius. Nobody even knows whether the barber found the bones in the Pond of Dreams, or somewhere else. However, Kenneth Rijsdijk (remember him?) and his colleagues from *Dodo Alive* searched the waters of the pond as recently as 2006, and they found a treasure trove of bones. Subfossil. I enjoy saying that.

From the Horniman Museum in London you can download a model of a dodo to a 3D printer. Is that what you want to do? It's a long, long way from the Pond of Dreams, a long way from the times when I wandered along through the warm, wet, glaucous greenery, watching the skinny flamingos, bypassing the big old turtles, catching glimpses of bright parrots on the wing. Swallowing fruit. There was a drought, you know, and, thirsty and desperate, we all crammed into the lovely waters of the Pond of Dreams where our bones have been sweetly preserved like cherries in a bottle of syrup for four thousand years.

Pause, if you will, to absorb some of that information.

I have given you the faintest whispering spiderweb scintilla of an impression of the history of the species so far. It is safe to say there is an infinity of information available in what is called 'out there'.

The next step is the Comeback. Cockadoodlecomeback. It won't be long now. Stay tuned. Hope is a wonderful, feathered thing. I remember the pond. I remember the stones. I remember *all* the dreams. The parrots. The rats. Stay tuned. And I tend to imagine there is a choreographer somewhere in an upper room busily devising *Dodo Lake*. Oh yes. Cue the new Tchaikovsky.

Dodo Lake, Pond of Dreams, Here Comes the Past. *Dodo Lake*, starring live onstage the Comeback *Raphus cucullatus*. Believe me. It's going to happen. Oh yes, it's going to happen. Stay. Tuned.

FERTILE AND FAITHFUL

Note: The Tasmanian Tiger (*Thylacinus cynocephalus*) is an extinct carnivorous marsupial, believed to have died out in 1936. It was thought that the remains of the last one had been lost, but in 2022 the skin and skeleton were discovered in the Hobart Museum. Scientists of the 21st century hope to resurrect the animal, while many people believe it still lives in the dense, remote forests of the island. The official name for Tasmania today is lutruwita, and the name for Hobart is nipaluna.

The 4th of May 1862 Karoola

My Dear Anty Thea

Today is my birthday I am ten now.
Thank you for sending me the pincushion
you prommised me it is beatiful.
I have wished to have one like this.
I think you are magic you make
ones from the top jaw of tigers. His teeth
are very scary and the pink satin is soft
and pretty I am proud and excited you hid my
three big back baby teeth
inside the woolly pad and some of
my baby hair it is a nice secret.
Do you thik it is the jaw of the tiger
that eat the chikens and baby Ninas boot.
Ethyl says it is she likes to teas.
Anty Heli is making a little rug from
peces of tiger skins it is all soft with strips.
Papa shot some on Friday he looked in the
pouches but no babies. Mama keeps saying
all shall be well but she still cries sometimes.

Yours sinserly with loving XX
XX Aletheia XX

PREFACE

Thylacinus cynocephalus, apex predator of the Great South Land that came to be known as Australia, was a marsupial, carrying its young in a pouch. It roamed far and wide across the GSL for 30 million years, but 3000 years ago *Canis lupus dingo* arrived and took over, so that *Thylacinus cynocephalus* all but died out. It survived only on the small southern island of lutruwita, which had become separated from the mainland by rising seas.

CHAPTER ONE

AND the wolfish animal was tawny-golden, it was striped, and its tail was stiff, and its jaw could yawn a great curvature of width, and its teeth would tear the flocks to pieces so that blood lay brightly upon the penumbra of the fields of night.

2 And for many thousands of years it roamed freely, quietly, stealthily through the forests of the island of lutruwita.

3 Pictures of its likeness were imprinted on the walls of caves, and they became a part of the walls themselves.

4 Until one day the tall ships with white sails moved into the harbour, bringing pale men with strange voices in their throats and swift rifles in their hands and rapid murder in their red-coated hearts.

5 And there came another day, in the Common Era 1936, when the last known tawny-golden animal lay cold and stiff and desolate on the dust of the floor of its small lonely cage in the zoo in nipaluna. Its sad old body was discarded.

CHAPTER TWO

AND the International Union for Conservation of Nature's Red List of Threatened Species was established in CE 1964.

2 And it came to pass in CE 1986 that the *Thylacinus cynocephalus*, pouched animal with dog head, tawny-golden, striped, was marked extinct on the IUCN Red list.

3 And this was seen as an official date, a truthful notice of the extinction of a species that is also known as the Tasmanian tiger, apex predator.

4 And, from that day forth, the people of lutruwita have suffered from the tears that flow with the shame, the guilt, the grief, the sorrow, the hollow darkness of the slaughter of a species.

5 For many bleak years of the late Anthropocene Epoch, the tiger was to science a long-lost animal. But lo, it lived on in the land of memory and imagination as a ghost, a myth, a fairy tale, haunting the deepest forests of the island, an elusive shadow of a living, yawing beast.

6 And in the secret Stygian night of the remotest forests of lutruwita, blood ran forever warm in the veins of the unseen tiger, who lived on in mystery and in perfection.

7 Rare wanderers, priests known for madness by the scientists known for clarity, produced photographs and documents and files and encyclopedias of evidence of the nocturnal rare realities of the wild dream-tigers of lutruwita.

8 "Handcart Harry's Hall of Hallucinations" was the title given to a story printed on the wall of one priest's house in the year CE 2022. And, on a rock wall where silent sketches of the dog-headed pouched animal lay embedded for all eternity, a bold hand wrote the word, and the word was 'Symbiocene', the time when all life on the planet is treasured and nurtured by humans.

CHAPTER THREE

AND there came a day in the year CE 1917 when the king of a far country decreed that the island of lutruwita would have a badge, a symbol, a coat of arms.

2 And lo, upon the badge there appeared a scarlet lion, a sheaf of wheat, a golden ram, shiny apples, and fruity hops.

3 And upon either side of everything, balancing on their hind legs, appeared two of the tawny-golden animals,

Thylocinus cylacephalus, their tails stiff-stretched, their dog-heads held up at a proud and noble angle.

4 And their names were written: Ubertas and Fidelitas. Dead and Gone, yet Fertile and forever Faithful. The image of the badge appeared on coffee mugs and silver spoons.

5 And back and forth the story shifted as the shape-shift of the animal moved from forest to laboratory, back and forth and back and forth.

6 And a plan was made to grow a shiny new version of the great stripy animal within the being of a tiny little browny grey *Sminthopsis*, known as a dunnart.

7 And in those days, there was a common saying that was 'follow the money', but in the case of the dunnart and the tiger, the money itself, many many millions of golden coins, began to follow the strange marriage, dancing along in the pockets of delirious and magical scientists.

8 And in the almost fullness of time the scientists became gods.

9 Until in the absolute fullness of time there came a day when, in a splash of synchronous miraculosity, the scientists announced the success of all their diligence and effort, while Harry the Hallucinator walked out of the forest with a sleeping tiger in his arms.

10 And so, Ubertas and Fidelitas were made from the ghostly mysterious mushroomy depths of the darkest fairy forest, and from old and new Deoxyaribonucleic Acid plus a great golden pool of golden golden golden coins.

11 All shall be well, and all manner of thing shall be well.

12 For the beauty and the wonder of it all was that Ubertas was a female animal, while Fidelitas was male, and the future of their family was secure.

CHAPTER FOUR

AND while the floods and the fires and the famines and the plagues ravaged the planet, and laboratories and museums and palaces toppled into the crimson seas, there appeared a child who climbed the gleaming marble stairs of the Palace of the Future. This child was the last child on the planet. And the child was dying.

2 And in the child's hand there was a box, and in the box a strangely pristine example of the ancient art of pincushion-making.

3 And hidden within the pincushion within the box were the child's distant ancestral teeth and also its distant ancestral hair.

4 With perfect hope in its faltering heart, and with tears of expectation in its dimming eyes, the child placed the pincushion upon the Golden Table of the Future from where it was sucked into the Great Machine.

5 And as the child lay in extinction, the noiseless Great Machine began its long and eerie and pre-determined process. From deep within the fluffy woollen womb of the soft pink satin pouch, Old Teeth and Old Hair began their journey toward the production of the Great and Golden Form of the Penultimate Series.

6 And all will be well.

IT'S A MOSQUITO THING

Don't you just love poplar trees? The old Greek story is that the seven daughters of the sun god, mourning the death of their brother, transformed into poplars and wept tears of amber. The origin of amber. That's a myth, but I am going to tell you a true story. It covers a great deal of time, beginning in the mists of time, with the amber bit.

Ninety-nine million misty years ago, or thereabouts, when insects were being trapped in amber, one of those insects was a species of fly, a 'mosquito', which is just a funny Spanish word for 'little fly'. If you prefer the Latin, here it is: *Culiseta longiareolata* .

Got that? Yes, six lo-ong slender legs, and a pair of wings that zzing and ssing and whiine in the warm air as Mozzie hunts for blood, preferably sweet type O. *Oh-Oh-Oh-Oh!* When they are not whining, they like to sing a little bit. That mosquito in the amber was my distant ancestor. Very very *very* distant, you would have to say. Moving swiftly along the family poplar—zhzh-ing—I take you to events in Egypt thirteen hundred or so years before even Jesus was born. I hope you can follow all these flights back and forth over the centuries.

In the land of Egypt there was a king—he was young and powerful and extra rich. So much gold and jewellery, you just can't imagine. You will have heard the wise words from James Shirley's old poem: 'Death lays his icy hand on kings.' It happens. Well, when the young king was nineteen, death did just that, and the king, suffering from malaria, passed into eternity. Now, you certainly know who delivers malaria, don't you? Zhzh-ing! It's a lady mosquito. I probably should have said that I too am a female—we're the ones, not the boys, that land on the skin and bite, to suck the blood and deliver the various pathogens. Vectors, we are vectors of parasitic diseases!! Vector rhymes with hector, and mosquito rhymes with veto. I like poetry, but I don't have much time to read or write it because we live for only about two weeks. I won't bother with a ditty. Time, you might say, is short. And there is work to do. More human deaths can be laid at our door than at the door of any other animal taxon. You'd better believe it. We do it because we have to get the blood to make our eggs. It's not really our fault if we deliver the fevers when we drink the blood. But to tell you the truth the family is riddled with guilt about all these deaths.

The name of the poor young king I was telling you about was Tutankhamun. He's incredibly famous, having been discovered with his glorious treasure after being entombed for over thirty-two hundred years there in the Valley of the Kings. You heard right. Thirty-two hundred years. Was that eternity for him? I don't really know. But on 17th of February 1923, after all those years, the final seal on the king's burial chamber was broken, and the eyes of all the world, so to speak, were on King Tut and his gleaming, pristine riches. Everywhere, the glint and glimmer of old gold. There has never been a news story like it, before or, I might venture to suggest, since. You could say it blew the universal mind. People have more or less forgotten the girls who turned into poplars and wept those tears of amber, but *everybody* remembers Tut-tut.

The treasure lives in Cairo, but parts of it sometimes travel the world. Tut's mummy and his sarcophagus are still in the burial chamber, and you can go and see them if you wish. But lots of other stuff is available to travel, and a museum anywhere in the world just has to whisper the word 'Tutankhamun' and wave some cash, to make a little fortune of its own. Zhzh-eengh! From beneath the warm dry earth in the Valley of the Kings goes something like the treasure—out, out to the bullet-proof display cases of the world. Maybe it will, in due course, travel to the moon. Most things will, I imagine. Will I, you wonder. Well, several members of my family have attempted to stow away in various rockets, but as far as I know, with no success. It's only a matter of time, since we rarely give up. Zzingoh!

Bright shining wall-paintings, larger than life, illustrating scenes from *The Book of the Dead*. Chariots, chairs, coffins of solid gold. A golden throne. Musical instruments, silent across the sweet millennia. Jewellery to die for. Seven oars to row the boat that ferries the king across the waters of the Underworld. There's a breastplate, decorated with four amber beads, meant to be placed over the heart of the king as a form of protection. Not particularly effective, you'd have to say. May I quietly remind you my own ancestor started all this when she delivered that little old malaria bug. I said just now that we are guilty, but obviously I for one am also proud of the cascades of consequences from the original bite.

Now coincidence is an interesting phenomenon and, as the tale unfolds, coincidence will play its smiling part. You would realise that a great deal of effort, and particularly mountains of *money*, must have gone into the search for, and discovery, of the tomb.

Far far away from the Valley of the Kings, in the English county of Hampshire, stands Highclere Castle, seat of the Earls of Carnarvon. If you happen to have seen any of the TV series *Downton Abbey*, you will know what that particular castle looks like. It was George, the fifth Earl, a keen amateur Egyptologist, who sponsored the expeditions that eventually revealed the glory that was Tut. Follow the money backwards and you come to the mighty wealthy Alfred de Rothschild, Director of the Bank of England. He was the indulgent father of a love child named Almira, and *she* was the American heiress wife of George, our fifth earl. I kind of wish she had been called 'Amber', but I suppose you can't have everything. Almira will have to do. Her father's money is what really matters here.

Now, the intense excitement of the Tut revelation was exhausting for the earl, and so after the tomb had been opened, he took a relaxing cruise along the Nile. As you do. In the warm air of the early evening, as the crimson sun was sinking in the west and, as the lazy waters lapped against the houseboat, there came the warning whine of a little zhzhzh-ing. Mrs Mozzie landed elegantly on the surface of the left cheek of Lord Carnarvon. She took a nice sweet drink of the good earl's bright blue blood. It might have even been a draft of sweet type O. One can only hope.

Such a teeny-tiny itchy-witchy wound. The next morning, as he scraped his face with his ivory-handled razor, Lord Carnarvon nicked his noble skin so that more blue blood trickled out. Bacteria, the first life-forms to appear on Earth, now made their way via the mozzie puncture into the good earl's bloodstream. There they go!

Back to Cairo he sails. Unwell. Days pass. Septicaemia. Gravely ill. King of England sends message of concern. Press bulletins every couple of hours. Fever. Pneumonia. Delirium. Death. By chance or fate the lights of Cairo fail. Blackout! Back home at Highclere, the earl's little three-legged dog Susie howls once, dies, and takes her place in history. Sad and marvellous coincidence.

Zhzh-ing! And the ancient poplars weep. They weep those tears of amber. And history tells Tut's grand old story, tells it over and over again, sometimes remembering the role of the mosquito, sometimes forgetting. But I can tell you now, it's a mistake to forget Mozzie, oh yes, a big mistake. Quite a bit of history is really just a mosquito thing.

SURVEILLANCE

Fact: Blowflies have the fastest visual responses in the animal kingdom.

I come from a family of showbiz, the arts, and the Church. We have been located in France, in Paris to be precise, for centuries. We are the Flies on the Wall. Also known as the Wall Witnesses, using our incredibly complex eyes to see into what are sometimes called Universal Truths. The family name is *Calliphoridae*. We also have perfectly beautiful geometric lacy wings and glittering bodies that can be seen to shimmer with magnificent shades of Prussian blue, of viridian, of amber and of vermilion. (Fancy arty colour talk.) My own main walls are in the small but grand, graceful, and gleaming church of Notre-Dame-de-Lorette, in the rue de Chateaudun—metro on rue Bourdalone. One of my favourite lookouts is the dome, where I like to settle high up on one of the small golden stars in a sky of lapis lazuli, beside the image of Notre Dame Herself. Blue and gold are the dominant colours of the light in the Lorette. Daylight floods down through the great glass cap in the top of the dome, spilling into the church, illuminating every speck of floating dust. Personally, I think the Lorette is much more beautiful than the sparkling sugar moonlight structure that is Sacré Coeur, viewed in all its glittery white splendour at the end of the vista from our front porch.

We have been about the world since time immemorial. Surveying the Pyramids of Egypt, busy around Stonehenge, working the forests of the Amazon, zooming about the deserts of Australia, working the decaying matter in the extreme reaches of the Arctic, following Marco Polo, Columbus, Napoleon—you name it, we were there on duty, breaking down organic matter, transmitting bacterial infections to animals and humans. Vectors of pathogens, that's us.

Of course, I am not always in the dome at the Lorette. I get out and about, but most often I see what goes on inside here, in the congregation, and behind the scenes as well. Sacred and profane. I just noticed a woman painting her fingernails blue while sitting quite close to the altar. Could it be some homage to the Virgin? I am not sure. She was pretty much covered in colourful, detailed religious tattoos. And the other day there was a young man who said to his companion: 'I'm just going home now to *think* about Oscar Wilde.' Oscar was known to visit the Lorette occasionally, so I suppose the remark was understandable. We *Calliphoridae* were here for the baptism of George Bizet and also that of Claude Monet. But of course, those events occurred long before the babies rose to stardom in the worlds of music and painting. But *we* remember. One of my aunts swears she witnessed a man in a brown overcoat stab a priest to death in the confessional. Nobody else has ever mentioned this event, and the problem with this particular aunt is that she is inclined to invent fantasies. These days the riot police in Paris somewhat resemble swarms of *Calliphoridae* in their burnished black armour, with their banks of shiny shields. We pass the tales of love, sorrow, crime, punishment and so forth down through the family. We gather a tremendous amount of information, and the stories keep us entertained after lights-out.

When the great old cathedral of Notre-Dame-de-Paris combusted in 2019, for some reason I sadly recalled a most tragic showbiz funeral we had here in 1863, and I now intend to share the story of it with you, because it is preying on my mind. Not just the funeral ceremony, which was the end of the story, but the life and times of the deceased. She was a ballerina, and several long-distance ancestors had witnessed her performances at the Opera. The Fly on the Wall during the obsequies was one such ancestor, and the tale is, I warn you, terribly, terribly sad. Whenever I tell such a story, I channel the relevant ancestor, so it sounds as if I personally witnessed the event. But I didn't.

Livry, Emma Marie, 1842–1863

The name of the deceased was Emma, a young ballerina at the Paris Opera, described in the press as being ethereal, intangible, diaphanous—as beautiful as a falling snowflake. She would bound and leap as if fashioned from the air itself, skimming over surfaces like a feather on the breeze. She danced the Sylph in *La Sylphide* in 1862, the year before her death. She also danced in *Le Papillon* where she was the heroine who was transformed into a butterfly. When the fluttering bright butterfly flew too close to a naked flame, it became a waltzing girl again, and she was able to marry the prince.

This was a truly terrible irony, since when Emma was rehearsing *La Muette de Portici,* life possibly, as they say, imitating art, her costume caught fire on a gaslight, and she died later as the result of her burns. 'Oh goodness heavens, no,' she had said when the dresser attempted to insist that she have her costume dipped in a fire-proof substance, dulled by safety, 'I will never use that stinky stuff. See how stiff it makes the skirts. I need air, I need air all around me to leap and fling and fly!' She felt the softness of the skirts, their flowing fabric, brushing against the smooth pale skin of her legs. As she entered the stage in the second act, she shook her skirts once too often near the lights and whoosh! Three times the little flaming torch on magic feet darted across the stage until she was captured by the firemen who rushed to save her. She clutched the burning fabric to herself in an attempt to hide her nakedness. It took months of agony and infection for her to die. Her slender whalebone stays, said the doctor later, were welded to her skin and she died from the poisoning of her blood. I always mean to visit the Musée de l'Opéra to see the charred scraps of her costume, but something seems to hold me back. Could I bear to contemplate the melancholy of those fading scraps? The clouds of incense at the Requiem billowed up, up into the dome, twisting, drifting in the pale sunlight. The coffin was draped in deepest velvet black, heaped with nosegays of muguet for this little lily of the valley in her mortal rest.

While the plots of ballets can be rather absurd— and believe me, I have been to the Opera myself often enough and have observed them at close quarters—the scene at Emma's funeral was pure tragedy, echoing as deep and as high as tragedy can ever reach.

Members of my family accompanied the faltering black clip clop of the mournful carriage from the Lorette to the Cimetière de Montmartre, and some of them never returned. We mourn for them, but we comfort ourselves with the image of them there at the graveside.

A requiem cloud of shimmering wings. On occasion I visit the spot to contemplate the flat and brutal slab of stone that lies atop the remains of the ballerina. A large plain cross of stone lies flat on the surface of the slab. The lichen and the weather have softened the simple statement of Emma's name and her dates. I find further comfort in the aromas of the graveyard. And I imagine that in the patterns of the lichens I can perceive the images of lily of the valley.

I witness plenty of funerals—not so many weddings and baptisms in these times of raving secular beliefs and uncertain gender—and sometimes, as I watch from up here, I tell myself the story of the original miracle to which our church is dedicated. If I didn't live here, I might like to live in the Basilica Della Santa Casa in Loreto, Italy. We had *Calliphoridae* on location when the miracle occurred. Naturally. It was long ago, when the stone house in which the Virgin had been living in Nazareth was flown by angels and deposited in Loreto, after a couple of stops along the way. The basilica in Loreto was built to contain the house. And our Paris church is named in honour of the miracle, which is a miracle that particularly appeals to us because of the role of the angels in transporting the house, angels being winged creatures not unlike ourselves. Well, I am exaggerating a bit there. Sometimes the Lady of Loreto looks after people (wingless) when they take to the air in various forms of aircraft. Sometimes she doesn't. I don't know how that works. We don't need her, I guess, but I do like to stay nice and close to her most of the time, here on my golden star, in the sky of lapis, high up in the shining dome, in the heart of this dear old city of Paris, watching.

There are things in heaven and earth that Siri and Google can't tell you. If you really want to know something, maybe consider consulting the Fly on the Wall.

THE AFFAIR AT THE RITZ

Speaking as a dying cockroach, I tell you it is nice to have spiders and insects like you to talk to. My voice is faint and muffled, but I know you can hear me, and I sense your sympathy and kindness. I know you would help if you could. I am reasonably philosophical, but tonight has been almost too much for me. Tonight, I have discovered that I am unable to face death calmly. I do not want to die.

I have lived in this bathroom all my life, raised a large family with hundreds of descendants all over the hotel. Two years ago, I was Grandmother of the Year. We always have a huge re-union in the kitchen on Christmas Eve, and next time, I won't be there. I can't bear to think of it—the sea of shiny backs and handsome feelers—and I will never know it again.

It's because I'm getting old, slowing down, that I'm in my present state. Once upon a time I could anticipate a human visit to my bathroom, even before the human thought of it. But tonight, she turned on the light and there I was—marooned on the tiles, halfway between the bath and the hand-basin.

She hated me with a radiant hatred. She must have realised I knew all about her, and she hated me for that. She was, of course, frightened of me too.

As far as she's concerned, I am a creepy-crawly, whereas she wears satin lingerie and goes to the hairdresser twice a week. She's in town for a brief holiday with her husband, but I have learned to sum people up in no time. I've got her number, and she damn well knows it.

Her holiday consists of shopping and eating and drinking, going to the pool and the sauna and having massages. Once she had her horoscope done. Her husband tries every now and then to interest her in the theatre—they went to the ballet and the opera, but she drew the line at experimental plays. I adore that kind of thing myself. You may have realised from my voice that I spent my teenage years studying elocution—speech and drama—that kind of thing. Once I went to the University in the pocket of a leather jacket and saw some students doing King Lear as flowers and vegetables. And another time I arrived at the Opera House in a velvet handbag. I heard Joan Sutherland.

Occasionally this woman goes out with her husband to humour him, but mostly her holiday consists of little trips to the boutiques and the antique shops, and then a drive to the beauty shop to have her nails done—then off to lunch.

Food is her main topic of conversation, actually, what she has and has not eaten. She says she eats the salad and not the strawberry shortcake. I wonder sometimes about that. Her figure is beyond repair, beyond belief, and must surely frighten other people in the sauna.

Oh, why was I so slow and stupid? I was having a lovely stroll along the green arabesques when on goes the light and in she comes to cleanse her face. Creams and lotions and moisturisers and all the rest of it. She is definitely not a good advertisement for Estée Lauder. Did I mention her boyfriend? He had just left, and she was moved to rush into the bathroom and remove her face.

What happens is: Husband goes to the opera; boyfriend arrives with flowers and wine; lady and boyfriend laugh and drink and hop into bed; boyfriend leaves taking empty bottle; husband comes back. 'Frank and Julia sent flowers,' she says.

You see I do know all about this woman. And she has done for me.

We both stood still and looked at each other for quite a long time like beasts in the jungle. But I was defenceless.

She reached for her husband's spray can of shaving foam. She squirted a great white cloud of the stuff on me so I could see nothing and I could barely move. Then I think she put a glass over me, slid a piece of cardboard under the glass. Trapped. She wrapped the whole thing up in a plastic shower cap, took out the glass, sealed the little parcel with a rubber band.

And now I am in the rubbish tin under the vanity unit. Waiting to die. It's a comfort to have friends like you with whom to share the final moments.

COMPLETING THE 1080 PROJECT

I have recently taken it upon myself to work my way through the internet in search of my ancestry. I call it my 1080 Project. As a wise old tech-savvy male elder of the family *Rattus rattus* and, with no chance of a pleasant natural death, I'm planning to avail myself of our voluntary euthanasia as soon as I've completed the project. I have access to that excellent metabolic poison, 1080. And at least we're never likely to go extinct like the poor old dodo. We were largely responsible for that particular vanishing you know. We travelled on the Dutch ships, and we rushed ashore on Mauritius and hopped into the dodo's eggs. The sailors also helped by killing and eating the big old birds. Wipeout!

I have been led hither and thither electronically, and now I will share with you some of the information I have unearthed online. There's the relationship I discovered between my family and a rather lovely seventh century Belgian saint, Gertrude. She is the only saint who has been accorded rodents as her emblem. First it was just the mice, the little fellows, but then we were permitted to participate, and Saint Gertrude is now the Patron Saint of the Fear of Rats. She is one of those saints who is not recognised by the Vatican. Mind you, there are plenty of rats in the Vatican. There's a popular Rattus boy-band called Squealing and Dealing that plays regular gigs in the kitchens. I just hope they can travel to perform at my funeral.

I, like most members of the family, am a zoonotic vector of certain pathogens, notably the Black Death, or bubonic plague. This disease is spread in two ways: by infected fleas from rats, or by contact with the bodily fluids of a dead plague-infected person or animal. It's kind of hard to know the answer to the chicken and egg question in this case. There's the rat flea and there's the rat. Rat carries plague bacteria, flea feeds on rat, flea bites human. Did the flea get its measure of bacteria from a rat in the first place? Or did the rat get its juice from the flea? Anyhow, the bacteria, once it pops into the bloodstream, travels to a human lymph node or two, where it reproduces, causing swelling. Painful. You bet. What follows is—now get this—necrosis of the extremities, the appearance of black dots and bruising, fever, cramps, seizures, bloody vomit, delirium, death. Fascinating. Those fellows online know their stuff.

As you would realise, the plague played its part in history, changed societies wherever it went. It's a matter of considerable family pride that it was one of us that carried the flea that bit Elizabeth, Queen Consort of Edward the Fourth of England in 1492. Maybe you can't place Elizabeth in the history you're familiar with. Well, I'll tell you. She was the granny of Henry the Eighth. Got that? She came from the House of York, the one with the white roses, and she was known as the White Queen. Oh, and she was the mother of those boys that disappeared in the Tower of London. She was quite pretty, if you can believe the portraits. I like to believe.

I'm fond of art, generally. You should see the statue of Saint Gertrude in Berlin. It's a big bronze thing on the St Gertrude bridge, and she's offering a boy a mug of beer. He's got a big goose with him—and—running around beneath his feet there's a ring of great bronze rats—and a few mice. Since people are frightened, they make up stories and legends about us, often with a grain of truth. Speaking of grain, we have sometimes changed the course of history by gobbling up all the crops. As for the legends—think of the Pied Piper of Hamelin— that's based on a true story. He musicked the rats away and, when the city refused to pay him, he musicked away the children. Interesting! Humans do go in for revenge and retribution. I always wonder where the rats and children ended up. They couldn't vanish into thin air, could they. Or maybe they could.

A significant rat death occurred in the royal palace of the Russian Emperor Peter the Third in 1762. The emperor had a big collection of toy soldiers, and used to organise scenes of warfare all over the floor. Well, one of my ancestors was making a meal of two delicious little cork sentinels who were guarding a fortress when the emperor's dog caught him at it and delivered him to the emperor. The emperor sentenced the old ancestor to death, constructed gallows and executed him. Quite a good way to go.

It doesn't matter where I look on the internet, there are traces of the *Rattus* family. It's amazing. And we simply love the way the planet's heating up. They used to say that in New York City you were never more than twelve inches away from a rat. That's a great overstatement these hot days—it's now more like six inches. We are closing in. Same in London. We're even closer in Paris and Rome. By the time the planet boils, we'll be half an inch from your ear. Nibble-nibble like a mouse (rat). There goes your ear. It really surprises me that they don't properly canonise Saint Gertrude to put her more firmly in the frame when it comes to fear of rats. Not that it would do them any good, mind you. We are organised, ubiquitous, invincible. But I realise it gives humans comfort to imagine they have a powerful good woman on hand to deal with us.

I plan to travel to Berlin to die at the feet of the statue of Saint Gertrude with whom I've become a bit obsessed. It wasn't until I discovered her that I made my final decision about the 1080. Does that sound a bit extravagant? I've always been known for the dramatic gesture. I will pack a bag with the precious white powder, bid farewell to the family at the cheese and butter factory, and take a jet to Germany. I hope I can organise to have Squealing and Dealing to play at the ceremony. Saint Gertie, here I come.

THE COCKATOO'S QUESTION

Cast of Characters
Caca the cockatoo
Lala the lapwing
Kaka the koala
Gaga the galah
Kookoo the kookaburra
Tata the Tasmanian devil
Fofo the fox

Caca: I have a question—I will get to that. Much of the time I hang out in the tops of the gum trees around here. I flatter myself that I'm like a great white sulphur-crested angel up here observing and commenting. (My full binomial name is actually *Cacatua galerita*—quite pretty, don't you reckon?) Believe me, I can see for miles. Talk about three hundred and eighty degrees!

Far and wide, far and wide. Habitat Househome here is the hilly bushland surrounding a little enclave of handsome new split-level brick househomes with triple everything—glazing, garages, insulation, flush toilets, soap, triple layer chocolate-orange mud-cakes, triple rows of pearly-pearls, triple-cut sim cards. I call them Triple Trill houses.

Once upon a time we used to be able to feast off the woodwork on houses—windowsills, door frames, lattice trims—but these babies are fortified against us. No fun. But handsome, don't get me wrong—they are the latest in Looks. As well as checking out the horizon, I get to see a fair bit of what goes on close to home, very close to home. Of which, more in a moment.

The big—and I mean big—story lately has been the hellfires whipping up and taking off all over. The messages coming in here have been, well, apocalyptic. *And death and hell were cast into the lake of fire*. You see, although I am planning to tell you some interesting domestic anecdotes, my mind keeps coming back to the state of the country. And I am inclined to recall words from the Bible. I can't help it, because the messages do keep coming in, and the smoke of the fires blows in, and the dust blows in, and they blot out every bloody thing. The bright blue sparkle of the enchanting lazy swimming pools beside the Triple Trills are murky with red mud. Inflated mermaids and flamingos and unicorns loll helplessly at the edges of the pools and are burdened with terrible flecks of mud. Folks are covering their noses and mouths with these masks that cause them to resemble some kind of weird sick bird with sore and worried eyes.

Down in a scrape of earth at the end of a gutter, outside a Triple Trill where there is, I regret to say, a rather large aviary filled with all kinds of sad and troubled exotic birds, Lala the masked lapwing has her nest. The lapwing chicks are still young enough to need some family protection, so Lala and her husband are often on patrol. They are very accurate in their dive-bombing assaults on human beings who get too close to the nest. It's often quite hilarious. I once tried to tell Kookoo the kookaburra about this, but he didn't think it was funny enough for a laugh. No sense of humour, really. The lapwings like to eat worms and things—I find this a bit disgusting when I think about it. But to each his own. My brain is so evolved, of course.

One day recently I warned Lala that Fofo the fox (an introduced species) was patrolling the grounds of the Triple Trills. Lala said she wasn't too worried because she had heard that Fofo was featuring in a YouTube video that showed her suckling the babies of a koala that died in the fires. This was such a turnaround of nature and was getting some humans very excited. They imagined the dramatic changes in the climate were possibly able to change the behaviour, even of foxes. I screamed at Lala.

'AS IF!' And then I said: 'It's fake news, you idiot. Who told you that crap?'

And she said Gaga the galah had told her.

I said: 'Lala, there's something you should know.' And I put her straight on the story, and on the character of Gaga.

I have little time for Gaga. She believes just about anything she hears. But she needs to draw the line at spreading rumours, particularly rumours as pernicious as that one. Fantasy foxes suckling the cuddly koalas. There are seven million red foxes in Australia as I speak. If even one of them started to turn into a lunatic nursemaid instead of a proper apex predator, it would be swiftly destroyed by its own kind. And long before a creature with a mobile had time to film it and put it on fucking YouTube.

I sent Gaga a message telling her to cease and desist. She did. But I will need to keep an eye on her. And I instructed her to apologise to Kaka the koala whose whole family had been wiped out when the eucalypt forest over there by Lake Lingaroo went up. She said she would apologise, but added an unnecessary comment to the effect that baby koalas not only drink their mother's milk, but also consume her excrement. Too much information! She can be nasty a piece of work at times, that Gaga. It's no use saying live and let live—it's a jungle out here.

Which brings me back to Lala and her chicks and Fofo who patrols the neighbourhood. Some of the human beings in Triple Trills leave out water and various sorts of food for the birds. Fofo is in fact partial to some scraps of soy and seed superloaf toast with unsalted butter and salami that regularly appears on the bird-table. It will not surprise you to know that the organic flour in the superloaf is triple-milled. The fact that Fofo is darkly yet brazenly lurking close to Lala's nest means that the chicks are definitely in danger. Not only from Fofo but also from bloody YouTube, I reckon. It could be just a matter of time before those relentless paparazzi Mr and Mrs Aviary Clever-Clogs gleefully pop a sequence online, showing the exact location of Lala's nest. This means Fofo doesn't even have to use her famous nose—she can just google, and hey presto! No more baby lapwings.

What we need is a good old Tasmanian devil such as Tata. It was her kind that wiped out the red foxes from Tasmania way back when. Mind you, there are reports of sightings of foxes in Tasmania in recent times. Can you believe it? And anyway, Tata's species is on the endangered list, mainly because of disease. And for that matter I wouldn't care to meet Tata in an alleyway on a dark night. That jaw! Those teeth! You've never seen anything like it. The natural world is a mighty complex setup.

There I go again, descending deep into woe, into the garden of gloom and the despair of everything. Babylon etc *shall be utterly burned with fire*. That video, of the fox and the 'koalas' might have been somebody's attempt to achieve a happy ending to a terrible story. It didn't do that of course, but maybe it did emphasise the need for tales of hope and nobility. And the need for change. Dramatic change. If the climate of the planet has changed for the worse under the watch of the Clever-Clogs, then the Clever-Clogs must be forced to change. I could tell them a thing or two. Obviously. They would never listen, of course. They think I am just a part of the comedy of nature.

BUT, is it possible that, in the happiest of all endings, *Cacatua galerita* might just lead the way? Four and twenty of us *clothed in white raiment and wearing crowns of gold*? Somebody once saw us in a vision. Oh where is that visionary now?

I can tell you now, **there is something you should know**.

My Question: What could that something be?

THE CARETAKER'S DAUGHTER'S DOG

That's me, Woffie the dog, a small animal of mixed breed with enough papillon for me to have great-looking ears, and enough Jack Russell for me to catch a rat. Parts of me shine golden in the sun. I choose to think I have a whole lot of papillon in me, mainly because I like to imagine myself as a bit of a 'continental toy spaniel'. What a lovely mouthful. Daphne is the daughter of the late Caretaker of St Blaise's little old church, bluestone, on the edge of the Melbourne CBD. We have each other, Daph and me. That's all we have, but it's enough. For us. I should make it clear, right here and now, that we are very happy. In case you were wondering. Or I could say 'reasonably happy'. The need for this modification will possibly become clear when I tell you we spend the day on the pavement outside the Dolce & Gabbana shoppe in Collins Street. Daph sleeps all day while I man the wooden box she uses as a begging bowl. Well, for the time being we're here, but in our profession these things never last. 'C'est la vie,' says the continental toy spaniel. If you come looking for us, we might not be there, might have moved on to pastures new.

You could be wondering how the caretaker's daughter became the woman on the lolly pink mattress on the pavement outside D&G. Well, you would be forgiven for going back to that old old song about who takes care of the caretaker's daughter when the caretaker's busy taking care—is the title copyright, or can I just come out and say it like that? It seems to me to be completely relevant, particularly since I have the perfect response to the question of who takes care. Obviously I do. Woffie takes care of Daph, and Daph takes care of Woffie. Like I said, we have each other. And, well, the Caretaker has shuffled off this mortal coil, and since he left no funds behind to speak of, and since it wasn't possible for Daphne to continue to live in the three rooms behind St Blaise's, we set sail together, and after a few years of trying to make a go of things in the city, we gave in to temptation and settled here, on the pavement outside Dolce & Gabbana.

Now most of the Passers-By are seriously fixated on passing by in shiny shoes and navy suits with silver buttons, but the few who hesitate are inclined to drop paper money in the box. When they do, I pick up the note and jump over Daph and tuck it in under her left shoulder, safe as houses. Sometimes, when handsome lady tourists from afar see me perform this trick, they put forward another note from their bottomless genuine leather shoulder bags, and Bingo! Woffie repeats the performance. How they smile and laugh and go on their way refreshed. Nobody has ever handed over a third note, but I imagine that one fine day, you know, they might. I think I said before that I have quite a bit of Jack Russell in me.

Going back to the three rooms behind St Blaise's for a minute—you wonder why some arm of the Church wasn't extended to Daphne, the Caretaker's Slightly Disabled Daughter when the caretaker had been finally taken care of. Well, you're quite right to wonder about that. Arms, bosoms, shoulders, hostels, shelters—oh, you name it, those things were offered, but part of Daph's condition is that she is a free spirit, and in fact she, with my help of course, escaped from the arms of the Church and the shelter of the shelters. It's a little mental disability she has, and most of the time you wouldn't even know it. Her mother? Ah, Mrs Caretaker died soon after Daphne was born, and thereafter Daph was her father's responsibility, and—well, you know the old song—who takes care etc. etc. If you don't know it you can easily get it on YouTube. She was forty-eight when her father died, and now I think she's fifty-two.

We must have been together, Daph and I, for about five years, but it seems like forever. We met one afternoon on platform ten at Flinders Street Station. It was deserted, and by some miracle, she approached from one end, and I came trotting along from the other and Bingo! We have been an item ever since, first of all in the Caretaker's rooms, and then out in the world. I have very little memory of my life before Daph, and what I do recall I try to forget. Let's just say I'm a Stray. Daph called me Woffie. She imagines we have a guardian angel, but I don't go in for that kind of thing myself.

Even though I have to be forever vigilant as Daphne sleeps her life away on the pavement, I must say I do enjoy the sight and sound of the trams sometimes sailing, sometimes trundling up, and down the hill, delivering hordes of careworn people to their places of work, love affairs, residences, entertainments, nourishments, worships and so forth. There's a nice cathedral just up the hill.

Sometimes I like to look in the window of Dolce & Gabbana. Oh my! Right now they are featuring the most amazing black and scarlet dresses, shoes, scarves, bags all thickly decorated with elaborate images of poppies. Like something from the battlefields of France, but elegantly glittering with gobs of jewels, and gleaming with golden thread. I have to be careful not to stare too long in the window, since my job is vigilance, and it's also doing the little dollar dance up over the sleeping body of my darling, tucking the crisp colourful notes under her shoulder.

Up above us, above D&B, above Christian Dior, above Montblanc, inside the grandeur of the gracious edifices, believe it or not, there are hundreds of people sitting with their mouths open in the chairs of hundreds of dentists while the dentists in white or pale blue coats drill and polish away. Nurses in pink and white flit about. Fine silvery tools clink and clunk onto bright porcelain trays. Sterile water swirls in miniature whirlpools. Like a great army of blowflies, the drills drill down into the little enamel jackets of a thousand teeth.

And here's a nice story: One time a dentist from up there came down in a rare moment of strange charity and, after he had deposited his five dollar note in the box and observed my antics, he said in a loud voice, 'Excuse me!' He bent over Daphne and kind of shouted. She stirred but did not wake. I barked. Five Passers-By jolted to a halt and stood there, bewildered, watching. It was a scene. 'Oh, excuse me!' the dentist said again. I growled. It's a pretty menacing low growl I have perfected and, believe me, I can do a lot of damage when I put my mind to it. Forget about human teeth and jaws, we're talking Jack Russell here. Then up strolled two handsome young policemen in those yellow hi-viz jackets, with every sort of weapon at the ready. The dentist desperately explained that he was planning to offer Daphne a free examination and treatment of her teeth and gums upstairs above the lovely scarlet poppy dresses and shiny poppy handbags. The police spokesperson—his eyes were cold and knowing—then quietly said it was better not to disturb the peace of the sleeping woman and her yapping dog. And the dentist then apologised to the police and went on up the street with his tail between his legs. (I made that up about the tail.) I smiled at the policemen, and the frozen Passers-By came back to life and did some more passing by. I felt a bit regretful about Daphne missing the chance to go up in one of the lifts to have her teeth done. I've seen a photo of her when she was younger—she had a lovely smile with a fine set of choppers, and a twinkle in her eye. Gorgeous auburn curls if I remember correctly. I even dreamt that the thoughtful dentist might be able to give my own teeth the once-over—and not before time, I can tell you.

So that's more or less a day in the life of Daph and Woffie. I take care of the Caretaker's daughter and she takes care of me. You might ask where we spend our nights, after our lovely days—what we do at night, all night, when the lights of Dolce & Gabbana gleam on like an hallucination, when the jewels on the poppy sandals glitter like the stars in the heavens above. Ask what we do when Daphne opens her eyes and feels under her shoulder and counts her blessings and packs

her bags and rattles my chain and we move slowly down
the hill at twilight towards the great Town Hall.

You can ask. But that would be telling.

THE TALE OF THE LAST UNICORN

Believe me, O Best Beloved, I am the last of my kind. I am not sure whether to say the last of my family, tribe, or species. It is really species, I believe. In any case, I have retired. Here in the far south-west forest of unimaginable beauty and secret depth—I refer to the impenetrable virgin woods of lutruwita—I plan to spend eternity. Now there is a somewhat marvellous concept, eternity. I understand it but I am unable to explain it. I think about it—being the last unicorn, I think about it a lot. In my thoughts and dreams I go drifting back to the beginning, but then the concept of the beginning is also no simple thing to explain, however I may be able to describe it. Bear in mind the fact that I am probably seven hundred years old. At least.

Once upon a time, the universe, if there was a universe, lay deep in slumber, dreaming of the beginning and the end, outside time, beyond space, just dreaming. There was no time, there was no space; there was dreaming, dreaming and sleeping, and no sound. Nothing was happening. But somehow, in this sleeping, dreaming, soundless stillness, something stirred. Or so I have been told. As I have indicated, my understanding is primitive, but I believe that by accident or by design, there came into being particles of light. And these particles of light dreamt their way together, and they must have collided, shattered, must have split into a million million tiny shards, shards of what can only be described these days as colours. Now if you can imagine a rope, twisted twine, plaited from all the colours in all their permutations and perambulations, you can begin to visualise the embodiment of the vast all-coloured female—for females as you know are mighty keen on colours. Yes, it was a female serpent. The first of her kind, well, to tell you the truth, she was the only one of her kind. Unique. Like me. I am the last and she was the first, and here we are now, in the woods of lutruwita. You thought I was alone; I did not mean to mislead you—I have the company of the Serpent, and we are known among ourselves—and we have only ourselves—as Unie and Serpie, or US.

Serpie has done incredible work in her time—and I do not mean to imply that her time is up—for US, time, you see, does not exist. Things are more or less as they were before the dreaming. There is no time as such, although throughout the earth all the creatures of sea and land and air, and also all the plants, all the seasons, are still moving and shining and kind of billowing as they perform the dreaming which goes on for eternity. There I go again, eternity. But I am attempting to describe the beginning, am I not.

Others have given me their accounts of the beginning, but the one I trust is Serpie who has the beguiling voice of a mother telling fairy tales at bedtime. She says she herself was the beginning, the mother of every living thing, emerging from the virtual nothingness in all her dazzling hues, and winding her way all over—all over!—the earth leaving sweet indentations and hollows until she finally returned to the first fissure, or place of her birth, and she suddenly found the ability to speak, to call, to conjure up another living creature. She called, and from the fissure, which had grown wide and weird in the time she had been away, leapt a whole family of bright green frogs! And she tickled them and soon they were laughing and leaping and gurgling and carrying on. And off they went all over the earth where lakes and waterways and seas appeared, and so came plants. Then out from the fissure, which was now enormous, flocked all sorts and kinds of animals—even birds and fish and so forth. Butterflies and bees. Imagine. And unicorns, naturally. And when it was ticking along nicely, Serpie sorted it all out with her rules and regulations, and any creature that disobeyed her was—wait for it—turned to stone. This was good because it gave rise to mountains and valleys, and they are useful in their way. I've been up to the top of some very high mountains, and I can tell you that the sight of the earth from up there truly is an inspiration!

It all sounds quite good, doesn't it, Beloved. But you must have begun to wonder, then, why Serpie and I have retired to the deep dark forest here at the End of the Earth.

All is not well in the world and, as I said, I am the last of my tribe. Serpie has got eternity in hand for herself, and she assures me she will extend it to me as well. Such power and generosity! She needs the company she says; it is extremely lonely here. And dark. Oh yes, it is very very dark. It so happens that the usual systems of the earth are shutting down one by one. Plague, droughts, floods, fires, famines. And the earth appears to have lost the will to regenerate. The lights are going out, I have heard, all over Europe. Oh, I remember Europe with such great affection. There was a time when I got to know the prettiest girls in France, Italy, Spain—those joyful bounteous countries lapped by the waters of the blue blue Mediterranean. Men on horseback with dogs and trumpets would spend their afternoons hunting for me in the forest. They would sit a pale and beautiful and spotless lady, young and tender, on a little silken seat in a glade where flowers dotted the grasses like red and orange stars. And they would imagine I would lie in the lap of the lady, overcome with enchantment. Then, they thought, they could shoot me with their arrows, and catch me in their nets, and—well I never really knew the end of the story—I think they planned to kill me and eat me. Eat me? Was that it? At a banquet in the vast hall of the nearby castle under the indigo sky?

I have heard tell that this is how many of my brothers met their fate, but I never knew what really happened when the men took the bodies back to the castle. I believe they used to keep the horn.

However, in my own case, it was thus:

I lived in the deepest part of the Forest of Paimpont where lie the Tomb of Merlin, the Fountain of Youth, and the castle of the Lady of the Lake. One day when I was very young, white as milk and soft as a baby swan, I was strolling carelessly through the dappled light beneath the great oaks and beeches, when I saw, sitting quite still in a pool of sunlight, a girl in a bright yellow— you might say golden—cloak. There were jewels in her hair. Her sweet head was tilted up to the sun, and I saw that she was blind. And she was weeping. Slowly, very slowly, I tiptoed up to her, and from behind the trunk of a vast and noble oak tree I whispered: 'Why do you weep, fair lady, why do you weep?' She drew in her breath and lowered her sightless gaze, moving her shoulders in a little shuddering gesture. I spoke again: 'Why do you weep?'

'My brothers have placed me here to die,' she said, in the voice of resignation and regret.

'I must die because of my blindness. No man will marry me, and I must die. Wolves will come and eat me. And so I weep.'

'If you will sit upon my back,' I said, 'I will lead you far away to a place of safety where your brothers will never ever find you. Will you come with me?'

'But who are you?'

I told her I was the youngest local unicorn, and she started up in alarm.

'But you must flee!' she said. 'Fly from this place because my brothers are out hunting, and they will kill you also.'

'Then,' I said, 'we must flee together.'

And we did, Best Beloved, we did. We journeyed for three nights and three days through rain and shine until we came to the lodging of an honest carpenter who offered us water and food and shelter. His wife gave the lady some sandals and a plain brown garment, for the lady had lost her slippers and her yellow cloak, and her green and violet silken dress was now in tatters. And do you know, we lived there in safety and happiness, meeting, from time to time, other pale and noble ladies from castles far away, ladies who were escaping from their brothers, husbands, convents. Until a great sickness swept over the land, and on one terrible, bleak afternoon the carpenter, the wife, their five little children and the lady all took the fever, and all died.

It was then that I began my lifelong dangerous journey across the dear planet on strange and untrustworthy vessels, over centuries, over seas, until I came at last, in recent times, to this haven at the End of the Earth where I met for the first time my dear and colourful companion Serpie who will take me with her into the great unknown forests of eternity.

That is the end of my telling of the tale, but the tale will go on and on until what is sometimes called 'forever and a day'. Here we dwell in forest darkness, just US, at the End of the Earth, Forever and a Day.

HUMANS AND ANGELS

SPEED BONNIE BOAT

From *The Chronicles of Carrillo Mean*

I am writing this story from a yacht off the coast of Western Australia, on my way to the island of Mauritius where I have been invited to undertake some historical research in the Sir Seewoosagur Ramgoolam Gardens. You may wonder why I would choose to go by water instead of air. Well, these days, water is safer than air. Hear me out.

I remember with a vivid pleasure the long hours I spent in childhood devouring the books in my grandfather's library, which contained what seemed to me to be an infinity of volumes. My grandfather was aptly named 'Philosopher Mean', and he was a prominent local character in the small Tasmanian mining town of

Woodpecker Point, near Smithton. I like to think I have in some ways taken up the mantle of Philosopher Mean, who died in 1960 at the great age of ninety-nine. His library, named the Charles Dickens Library in honour of my grandfather's favourite writer, was home to a broad collection of unpublished memoirs by people known and unknown to history. It was one of these, the short journal of a British-Australian soldier who was killed in the second battle of Ypres on 25 April 1915, that recently caught my attention. The soldier's name was Wilfred James Bryant.

The journal begins when Wilfred, at the age of twenty-four, took a ship from Southampton to travel to Tasmania in 1901, and ends when he was about to set off for the war in Europe. His original journey was undertaken in order to escape from the ravaged landscape of much of England following the failed invasion of creatures from the planet Mars late in the nineteenth century. Wilfred's family had died in the invasion, and he, a budding mining engineer, had decided to put the tragic and sorrowful past behind him and to begin a new life in Woodpecker Point. The poignant fact that his life was spared during the Martian invasion, only for him to die in battle in Flanders, struck me as being starkly ironic. (His case is not as ironic as that of the deaths of boys called Victory who were born on November 11th, 1918, and who died in the war that began in 1939.) Between the two terrible events—the Martian invasion and the First World War—Wilfred had become a respected and successful contributor to the Tasmanian mining industry. I searched for his details in *A Comprehensive History of Mining in Tasmania 1847–1910*, where I discovered the following entry:

> *Mr W.J. Bryant was born in Esher, Surrey,*
> *in 1880, and he studied metallurgy at the*
> *Mason Science College in Birmingham. He*
> *arrived in Hobart in 1901, transferred to*
> *the gold mine at Beaconsfield from where*
> *he later moved to take up a position at the*
> *mine in Woodpecker Point. Since that time,*
> *he has resided with the manager of the*
> *Golden Goose mine, Mr G. E. Bannister,*
> *and has worked as an assayer at the mine.*

The words were accompanied by a small, formal, oval black and white photograph of a handsome Wilfred, his eyes large and clear, his beard short and carefully trimmed, a slight upward curl at the ends of the dark moustache, the ghost of a smile on his lips. There is no explanation of what might have caused Wilfred to emigrate, the little paragraph leaving such matters to the imaginations of readers who might well have conjectured that he was lured to the faraway island by the promise of riches. Or could be he was adventuring in the wake of a heart broken by the refusal of his suit. Was there a shy or haughty young lady who had toyed with his affections? Personally, I imagine his life was so blighted by the tragedy of the loss of his parents and sisters in Esher, while he was safe in Birmingham, that he decided to proceed in the hope, or expectation, of a happier life, a better fate in the distant colony.

Wilfred's own journal does not refer in any way at all to the horrors of the Martian invasion that passed through Esher. It is as if he is a single organism sprung from the classrooms of the Mason Science College, ready to find his way, make his fortune, on the goldfields of this island. I consequently searched the shelves of the library for a copy of *The War of the Worlds* by H.G. Wells, which I re-read for the fourth or fifth time, on this occasion in search of scenes that Wilfred might have known. At the least they must surely have been experienced by members of his extinct little family in Esher. Perhaps he was not in Birmingham but in Esher when it all happened; perhaps he undertook a journey not unlike that taken by Wells' narrator.

This book is one of the fullest accounts of that curious, historic, unexpected, and devastating series of events of 1896. So far as I know, the first Martian invasion is the only earthly invasion undertaken by beings who were not of the planet Earth, and I commend *The War of the Worlds* to anyone who is interested in the phenomenon of invasion *per se*, something that is common enough to be 'natural' among the peoples of Earth.

In prehistoric times, the Celts invaded the islands of Britain. Romans, Vikings, Goths and so forth all left deep and indelible marks on the British Isles. Looking mainly at British history, you can trace the beginnings of the invasion of other countries by Great Britain back to the seventeenth century, and the founding of the British East India Company under Queen Elizabeth I. In fact, the name Great Britain was first used by King James I in 1603. But this is not the place for a full history of Britain's invasion and colonisation of other parts of the world. I will skip to the time of Queen Victoria; a time when the sun never set on the British Empire.

In 1803 the British established a military outpost at their New South Wales colony on the Derwent River in Van Diemen's Land, later known as Tasmania, and now officially named lutruwita. The plan was to set up a British camp run by soldiers and manned by convict-slaves in order to dissuade others, such as the French and the Dutch, from developing a base in the area. In 1644, the Dutch had already claimed the island when Abel Tasman's ship's carpenter swam ashore and planted the Dutch flag at Frederick Henry Bay, named for Prince Frederik Hendrik of Orange. Because my family has lived here for generations, when I hear the word 'invasion', I think, more often than not, of this invasion of the island by the British in 1803. To the people who had lived on the island for many thousands of years, this operation was less abrupt than the Martian invasion of England, but it was considerably more deadly, and was, of course, successful in that it gave the British dominion over a decimated population of an ancient race. Whereas the Martians quite quickly succumbed to bacterial infections, the British brought their bacteria with them to the island, as well as their gunpowder and their poisons and their cracked, convenient, and inhumane belief that the inhabitants of the island were dispensable because they were not really human anyway. Over time there developed a myth that the original people had been completely killed off, removed from existence by the genocidal operation of British imperialism. However, I myself am living proof of the blind inaccuracy of this legend, for my great-great-great grandmother was a member of the palawa peoples, and her blood is in my veins. So, what occurred here in lutruwita, was *unsuccessful* genocide.

There is a short section early in *The War of the Worlds* concerning the invasion of the place by the British.

I think it is best if I quote it here in full, since it is
an example of the determined perpetration of the
myth. Reflecting on the destructive onslaught of the
Martians, the narrator of the story says:

> *And before we judge of them [the Martian*
> *invaders] too harshly we must remember*
> *what ruthless and utter destruction our*
> *own species has wrought, not only upon*
> *animals, such as the vanished bison and*
> *dodo, but upon its own inferior races.*
> *The Tasmanians, in spite of their human*
> *likeness, were entirely swept out of existence*
> *in a war of extermination waged by*
> *European immigrants, in the space of fifty*
> *years. Are we such apostles of mercy as to*
> *complain if the Martians warred in the*
> *same spirit?*

Note the blind and chilling phrase 'in spite of their
human likeness', and the use of the term 'inferior
races'. I might remind my reader that in the official
government writings of Australia, and in the minds of
the invading colonisers generally, the ancient peoples
were, until recently, described and classified as being
part of the flora and fauna, not part of the human
population. But I must return now to the journal of
Wilfred the young assayer, for it is in this record that
I discovered, woven into the account of life at sea,

one of the most disturbing and alarming pieces of information you will ever hear.

On board the steam ship *Outhwaite*, he befriended the ship's doctor, Henry Swift, who was travelling to Hobart with his ten-year-old daughter, Mercy, and her governess, Adelaide Jones, his wife and two sons having been killed in Barnes during the Martian invasion. It is Mercy Swift who is in fact the real focus of my interest here.

According to Wilfred, Mercy was a dreamy, intelligent, engaging child who loved to play quoits, sew, read, and tease Adela Jones who was sweet, charming, long-suffering, with a cloud of soft brown curls, pink cheeks, and deep brown rather mournful eyes. Wilfred was clearly fascinated by Adela, while Adela was clearly in love with Henry Swift. I can add a footnote to all this, for I know Henry and Adela married in Hobart and raised a large family in a house I have in fact visited in Davey Street. If Wilfred knew of the marriage, he forbore to mention it in his journal.

Mercy and Adela shared a cabin on board the *Outhwaite*. And it was in this cabin that Mercy housed her pet white rat, a secret to be kept from the ship's authorities, although the captain, it seems, had his suspicions. There was also a precious box of dead insects from which Mercy could not be parted. She would take them out of their box and set them up on a table in the saloon and invent little stories about them. She was a prodigious storyteller, and in later life she wrote several books for children and illustrated them herself. The rat was known, somewhat unimaginatively, as Rattie. But it was another of Mercy's treasures altogether that captured Wilfred's attention, and, I have to say, mine. This was the dormant creature known as Buddie who lived, snuggled in a grey silk shawl, inside a battered leather satchel that Mercy kept with her little collection of books. Adela was unaware of the existence of Buddie, believing the satchel to be for the purpose of carrying some of the books and Mercy's embroidery cloths and threads. Indeed, it did also serve this purpose. However, folded carefully into the depths of the satchel was a sleeping, breathing creature which can only be described, in a language possibly unfamiliar to Wilfred, as a deadly time bomb. Buddie was an immature Martian on his way to the New World.

As the narrator of *The War of the Worlds* explains, the Martians are highly adaptable, being principally made up of one huge, round brain. They are able to alter their bodies as the situation demands, and they communicate telepathically with each other. Their young are produced by budding off from the adult body, 'just as young lily bulbs bud off'. In moments of danger these buds drop into a dormant state, waiting for the telepathic message from Mars for their instructions to wake up and take on adult characteristics and duties.

I will quote a section from Wilfred's journal. At the time of writing, he was recovering from a fever for which Henry Swift had treated him, and he was partly of the opinion that he was suffering from an hallucination.

"The child Mercy entered the cabin, carrying her leather satchel. She was humming the 'Skye Boat Song'; *speed bonnie boat, like a bird on the wing*. She has such a pretty voice.

'Are you awake, Willow?' she said softly. I opened my eyes and murmured, unable to articulate any sensible words.

She sat down on the floor beside my cot and proceeded to fish out her sewing. I perceived she was embroidering on calico an elaborate design of bees and pansies, and I recognised this as a pattern one of my sisters used to make. I uttered an involuntary sob as the thought of Agnes sitting by the fire with her needle flashing in and out, back and forth, purple and green, gold and black, roused in me a great sorrow at my present lonely state in this world. I closed my eyes as a few tears trickled across my cheek. Mercy continued her humming, and soon enough I recovered myself and lay there gazing at her. As I did so, she took Rattie from the satchel and placed him on her shoulder, where he perched quite peacefully. Then, putting aside her sewing, Mercy drew from the leather mouth of the satchel a bundle of grey silk, which she proceeded to unfold with great care and precision. Finally, lying on her lap was a sleeping creature, brown and slightly wrinkled, a great round head with two enormous hands, and no body to speak of. Its huge bulbous eyes were closed; it had no nose; a sharp beak-like feature served it for a mouth.

'Good morning, Buddie,' Mercy whispered. As she did so she sprinkled the creature with little handfuls of red seeds, which pattered onto its skin and settled in the folds of the silk. I almost sat up and, but for my fevered weakness, I would have done so. For I have seen those seeds before; they are the seeds of the red weed that proliferated across the south of England during the invasion. How can it be that this child is carrying around with her the very objects, animal and vegetable, that can destroy the world? Then she began to sing to Buddie. She sang the French lullaby, 'Fais Dodo', and I gulped and uttered another great sob and a kind of croak, for the song was one my mother used to sing to me when I was a child.

Mercy quickly flung the grey silk cloth across the creature in alarm.

'Oh Willow, are you ill again. Shall I call Papa?'

But I was speechless, and weak from the fever, and dazed by what I had seen, or what I had imagined seeing.

With the practised skill of a stage magician, Mercy methodically parcelled up her sleeping pet, her seeds, and her sewing, cupped her hand around Rattie, and slipped everything into the satchel.

'I think perhaps I should read to you, Willow. We were just beginning Chapter Three.' And she took from the pocket of her pinafore a soft paper copy of *Alice's Adventures in Wonderland*, and began:

'They were indeed a queer looking-party that assembled on the bank.'

I listened as if in a dream. What had I seen? What had I heard? I recalled the story of the young Martian that was born on Earth during the war. It had been still attached to its parent, having not quite budded off. And I heard that the scientists Charles Foster and Sir Percival Swope, in their exhaustive studies of the Martians, decided, or at least seriously speculated, that the young are able to exist in a dormant state outside the parent's body for considerable lengths of time, waiting until they are needed, fully instructed from and in communication with the authorities on Mars, for any contingency. Sir Percival wrote a paper, which was more or less dismissed as far-fetched and possibly deluded, on the possibility that the sleeping young could remain in a suspended state for, as he said, a hundred years.

And he likened this notion to the story of the 'Sleeping Beauty'. His reference to a fairy tale was mocked in the press and also in scientific circles.

Is it possible that I actually observed Mercy Swift remove from her satchel a sleeping baby Martian? The seeds of the red weed? Surely it is not possible. If I report this to her father, I will surely only prove to him that the fever has entered my brain and destroyed my reason.

I have decided to dismiss this whole episode from my mind. I believe it must have been a vision born of the fever and referring to the horrors and tragedies I suffered as a result of the Martian invasion. I will never confess any of this to a living soul."

Ah, is it wisdom or folly that compels human beings to confide in their journals?

I am now certain that what Wilfred dismissed as a fevered vision was something that truly occurred in that cabin on board the *Outhwaite* as it made its way to Hobart.

In December 2019, lutruwita was experiencing catastrophic floods and bushfires, in temperatures of forty degrees Celsius. My grandfather's library was the coolest, most comfortable place in Woodpecker Point, and so I spent many hours quite happily reading whatever took my fancy. For some reason I kept coming back in fascination to Wilfred's journal, to the page about the Martian bud in Mercy's satchel, to the part about the red seeds. And then …

My TV reception and internet connection here are not great, but on Christmas Eve I began to see intermittent disaster news items reporting the strange happenings in Davey Street, Hobart. A peculiar red weed had apparently grown up overnight in the garden of the house where the celebrated children's author and illustrator Mercy Swift had lived as a child. This house is now a kind of museum where they display Mercy's books, her toys, her sewing, and so forth. I have myself been there on one occasion, and it is a popular place with tourists and groups of schoolchildren. I think I might have observed the leather satchel on a shelf in a glass display case. Did it at the time still contain the sleeping Buddie in his silk parcel? The red weed was unstoppable by any method, chemical or physical. It had exited the garden and overtaken the road, blocking the traffic as people were attempting to drive to the cathedral at the bottom of Davey Street. The doors of the cathedral were open, and the red weed went marching boldly in where it completely filled the building, broke the windows, and continued on its rampage.

At first people thought the news items were some kind of bad-taste hoax. People these days are quite accustomed to 'fake news'. I suppose *The War of the Worlds* radio broadcast Orson Welles made on Halloween in 1938 was one of the first big fake news stories of recent history. But I realised the red weed story had to be true, and I feared there was worse to come. The direct slaughter of the people by the Martians, people killed in falling buildings, people succumbing to the poison of the black smoke. Wilfred's account of Mercy's visit, his view of Buddie and the red seeds, it was all true and hideously ominous.

What to do?

I needed a friendly and seriously receptive ear. I phoned Gustav Fortescue, who is an old friend and who works in the Geology department at the University of Tasmania, as it is still known, in Hobart. He was at the airport waiting for a plane to Canberra. I explained what I knew, and what I thought I knew. I imagined the scenario for him: it's time for the Martian invasion of Earth to begin in lutruwita. On Mars they have perfected a telepathic immunity, which is sent to Buddie so that earthly diseases are of no consequence to him. The instructions go out to Buddie who has been sleeping, yes, just like Sleeping Beauty, for over a hundred years. They activate the red seeds. Buddie gets going, poisonous black smoke billowing around him.

He produces hundreds of buds that leap into deadly life. Should Gustav call the police? The army? What would he say?

Gustav heard me out with a kind of unearthly patience. And then he said quietly, 'It's already happened. They have taken over the island. I am hoping to get to the mainland, although God knows, they are probably heading there. Get out while you can.'

I was fortunate enough to be able to charter an aircraft from Smithton to Perth from where I set off for Mauritius in the yacht. Of course, it is possible that nowhere on Earth is safe. Time will tell. Human life is perhaps about to go the way of the dodo that was hunted to extinction on Mauritius by the Dutch in 1681. You will have realised by now that the invaders have disabled the air routes. So, as Mercy sang to the dreaded Buddie all those years ago, I say: *Speed bonnie boat, like a bird on the wing.*

Carrillo Mean

January 2020

TWO THIRDS OF THE TRUTH

A tale from the collection *Yesterday Tomorrow Today* by Hepzibah Zangwill

ONE

In the north-west of the island once known as Tasmania, not far from the virtual ghost town of Copperfield, is the Van Diemen Flower Farm, one of the enterprises of the Mean family. In the late 1940s, after the war, Van Diemen became known for its tulips. I was at school in Hobart with Trixie Mean, until, early in the war, her family moved back up north to the farm, and I never saw her again. Like me she never married, and she ended up managing Van Diemen. If there is one childhood friendship that has hovered forever in my memory, it's this one. Something went out of my life forever when Trixie disappeared. We parted ways without really noticing, sometime during the Battle of the Coral Sea. My family was fixated on news of the war; Trixie's people were ardent pacifists. Several members of my family died in the Holocaust. In 1995, on September 21st, Trixie slipped into a flooded river, up there in the north-west, and drowned. Beatrix May Mean. She was sixty-five years old. I read the death notice, by chance, in the paper. Distant memories came surging back. I pride myself on being unsentimental, practical; could be I am more sentimental than I imagined.

The child Trixie was a storyteller, known for her vivid imagination. Those days, I was pretty gullible. I think I believed everything she said. I used to hear, in her stories, inklings and threads, like slow drifts of almost invisible smoke, echoes of visions and visitations that came to me just before sleeping, just after waking. I could have told stories too, maybe. I sensed there was knowledge that I almost possessed. It was the kind of knowledge to which Trixie had access, swift and sure. When she told me things, she painted pictures with her words, and I seemed to hear an angel speak, to see a magpie on a bicycle calmly riding by, a Mexican in hat and gumboots digging for buried treasure in the desert sand. Once, without any prompting from Trixie, I saw my grandmother turn into a pale blue butterfly. But it was many years before I began writing stories, years

I spent travelling, working as a librarian far away in Florida, until I came 'back home' to the island. Trixie had stayed on in Copperfield, supplying tulips to the public far and wide. We had completely parted ways. I wonder if she lost her storytelling habit? I wonder.

I always liked it that she often used my full name, Hepzibah, not Hep, or Hepatitis, like other people did. She said she envied me for having two zeds in my name— she had one x.

'Hepzibah,' she would say in a soft, slow voice, 'did I ever tell you about my grandfather's pet unicorn?'

'Don't listen to her. There's no such animal as a unicorn.'

But on she would go, and I would listen, and I would believe.

'They're in the Bible. Eloi, eloi, lama sabachthani,' and she would recite bits of Psalm 22, getting to the verse about the unicorn.

Chocolate, she said, flowed from the taps in her aunt Felicity's house in Copperfield. The thylacine that died in the zoo in 1936 was not the last thylacine of all. In the horizontal forests of the north-west there were secret herds of them. One of her other aunts kept them as pets, and when they died the aunt made pincushions from their jawbones. Trixie's eyes were green, her hair was long, curly, and deep, wild auburn, glowing in sunlight like the tail of a quick dark fox.

'Liar, liar pants on fire,' the other children sang. I remember I protected her, stood by her as she defied them. Her tales were never simple lies from everyday life. She wouldn't, for instance, say she had done something she had not done, or seen something she had not seen. She was completely straight about the everyday. She didn't believe in fairies; she *did* believe in angels. She said they were green, like trees. There was something distinctive about the lies, supposing they were always lies. My father was a lawyer, and he used to make pronouncements about 'the truth'.

'I want the truth, Hep,' he would say, 'not two thirds of the truth, the truth.'

'My aunt Dorothy has a flower from the First World War,' Trixie told me. 'Her sweetheart sent it from the Middle East, and it's all dead and twiggy, like a horrible claw. It's called the Rose of Jericho, and when you put it in a bowl of water for a while it opens up and comes alive again. Her sweetheart never came back. He died. And she's also got a dried-up old daisy called the Rose of Bethlehem too. It does the same thing. I don't know where she got that from. Maybe another sweetheart. It's on a silver bar so you can wear it as a brooch. Quite pretty when it opens, but when it dries out, it's just a dead daisy, you know.'

I didn't know. Or did I?

'My uncle keeps the head of the last Aborigine in a little leather suitcase. One day you could come to

Copperfield with me and I'll let you see it. It's called William.'

My own family, tired of these tales I brought home, was pleased when Trixie and her fantasies disappeared into the mists of the horizontal forest. I never told them about her distant relative who travelled in time, and much later when I read the story by H.G. Wells, I realised, or thought I realised, that Trixie's so-called family legend was simply some sort of re-telling of that narrative.

Her great-great uncle Phoenix, she said, was known as the Time Traveller. He came back to the present in about 1895, having been to the year 802,701 and then he took off again, never to return. As far as anyone knows. Trixie always said she was expecting him to turn up again. In Hobart? In Copperfield?

'Oh, definitely in Copperfield. His family are just about all there. All the ones that matter. Me. He will want to talk to me. Definitely.'

'But won't he be about a hundred or maybe a hundred and fifty?'

'Yes, but that won't matter.'

My parents disapproved of Trixie, and my brother thought she was simply mad.

I sometimes think, in a dreaming kind of way, that in another life Trixie and I might have become a couple.

TWO

Trixie's funeral was held in the charming timber tearoom at the flower farm. I decided, after all these years, to go, so I took a flight from Hobart to Burnie, a coastal town famous as the original home of Reflex copy paper. 'Always Rely on Reflex'. At the airport I hired a car to drive to Copperfield, which is tiny, but not such a ghost town as I had imagined. There were ruined timber houses covered in morning glory vine, vivid pink pig face cactus spreading across empty fields in which stood the remains of sheds or stables. A few handsome old stone buildings have been transformed into charming modern dwellings. There's a rambling rickety ancient general store where you can buy just about anything.

The ceremony for Trixie was small, quiet, and gentle, with a welcoming Quaker-ish atmosphere. Family and some friends from the local area. I think I was the only one who had travelled any distance, travelled from the distant past. At one end of the room there was a glowing fire, a comfort after the faint chill of the spring air outside. I had never in fact met any of Trixie's family before, but they knew me as her friend from long ago. Her brother Matthew presided, and it was clear that Trixie's death was a terrible blow to them all. On a low table were several photos: Trixie as a small child sitting on a piano stool, holding a white velvet rabbit; as an older child, wearing our school uniform; teenager, young woman, middle-aged, old. The vivid hair of youth had morphed into a cloud of white. The face seemed scarcely to alter as the years passed. There was a sweet, whimsical smile that flickered across each image. How horrible it was, that she had drowned.

The place was discreetly decorated with glass bowls of white and gold classic tulips. From the windows I could see row upon row of blooms, rainbows swooping and stretching towards the sky. Dazzling, hallucinatory. Afterwards, the pine coffin was buried in a field, alongside several other graves, each marked with just a small boulder. Beneath tall sheltering gum trees, Matthew, unaccompanied, sang the hymn 'One Heart, One Mind', and then a girl played the guitar and sang 'The Land o' the Leal'. There was something mesmerising and other-worldly about the whole thing. I could not reconcile the girl I used to know with the idea of the body of the woman in the coffin. She used to make up silly songs using lines from old poems or the Bible. Unicorns and lions. What was that thing she used to sing about unicorns and lions?

Afterwards we returned to the tearoom and had sandwiches and stroopwafels with tea and coffee. On one wall of the tearoom were Mean family photos in a variety of simple wooden frames, oval, square, rectangular. Some had names. A small man in a frock coat, with a short white beard, his hand resting on a pale stone wall, was labelled 'Phoenix'. This, I supposed, was the so-called Time Traveller. It seemed to me this was not the moment to begin asking questions. At the back of my mind, I half planned to return one day and attempt to find out more about Trixie's family's past. Facts. The truth?

As I was leaving to drive back to Burnie, Matthew stood by the car and handed me a small package.

'Trixie always said she wanted you to have this. I think it's something from the time you were at school together. Not sure what exactly.'

The parcel was wrapped in brown paper, and tied with string, and on it was written, in lovely copperplate, 'For Hepzibah Zangwill, who always believed in me.' Fifty or so years before this, I believed in Trixie. How and why did that really matter to her? I could scarcely believe my eyes, which filled with stinging tears, and if hearts break, I thought my heart would break. I could almost hear her distant girlish voice: 'Head in a little suitcase and his name is William.' Matthew handed me a large, red-chequered handkerchief, I dried my tears, and we parted. I placed the parcel on the seat beside me, unable to comprehend the fact that Trixie had reached across time to touch my unsentimental heart. Were her dreams perhaps my dreams?

THREE

On the road back to Burnie, in the gathering twilight, I almost ran over a pair of Tasmanian devils fiercely mating in the middle of the road, almost crashed the car as I avoided them. The parcel, the size of a paperback book, was so potent that I was unable to bring myself to open it until I got to Burnie, to a tired and dusty yet comfortable old hotel. Burnie was at the time in turmoil because if industrial strikes at the paper mill. 'Always Rely on Reflex'. I saw no sign of the strikes as I drove up to the Bass Strait Inn.

The hotel bedroom looked out over the forlorn and wild grey waters of the Strait. The mournful cries of seagulls echoed the feelings in my heart. The place was furnished with floral chintz and faded lace, and pictures of English country scenes. Cheap china dogs on a mantelpiece above the fireplace where a small fire was burning in the grate. Old world comfort. A tiny elegant bookcase filled with sad old hard-cover volumes that looked as if they might fall apart at a touch. Edgar Allan Poe, Jane Austen, *Dot and the Kangaroo*. Some cheap, paperback Agatha Christies. A Gideon Bible, a dictionary. The bed was covered with a pale green silk eiderdown from long ago. The exuberant pink roses of the carpet were faded to a blush. I sat at a small oak desk that was stained with ink and marked with scratches. I cut the string of the parcel with a pair of nail scissors I found in a drawer. The paper wrapping sat tightly around a plain brown cardboard box as if it had been in place for a very long time. I unfolded the paper carefully and lifted the lid of the box. Inside were three objects wrapped in soft white tissue paper. Each had a handwritten label: Rose of Jerusalem, Rose of Jericho, Weena's Flowers. So maybe the tales of the two roses were true. But Weena's Flowers?

Trixie had never told me she actually *had* Weena's Flowers—the flowers from the year 802,701. The flowers that Weena the little Eloi gave to the Time Traveller in the Wells story, the flowers the Traveller carried from the future to the present, which is now the past; the flowers he handed to the storyteller, the flowers he left behind when he disappeared into the future, never to be seen again. Weena's Flowers? Surely this was not possible. Trixie had gone too far. A joke? There was a short note addressed to me. My hands shook a little as I unfolded it. Again, Trixie's handwriting, which in fact almost mirrors my own rounded flowing script.

FOUR

For Hepzibah
Here are the magical dead roses I used to tell you about.
Also, Weena's Flowers, which a stranger sent to Aunt Felicity from London.
You will know what to do.
With all my love from beyond the grave,
Trix

I sat and stared at the flowers. They were flat and slightly crumpled, with serrated, almost frilled edges. The colour was a pale umber, thin as one layer of human skin, but strangely resilient. There were three of them, each bloom almost covering the palm of my hand. I remembered the Time Traveller had said they resembled mallow. The dictionary was no real help, its entry under 'mallow' being to me only a source of confusion. I would know what to do. Would I? Love from beyond the grave.

I remembered that Agatha Christie's married name was Mallowan. Then I thought I might take my mind off things by reading a bit of crime, since the only TV in the place was down in the lobby. I picked up *Sad Cypress*.

The first thing I read was the verse from Twelfth Night:
'Come away, come away, death,
And in sad cypress let me be laid;
Fly away, fly away, breath:
I am slain by a fair cruel maid.'

That only took my mood back into deep sorrow and regret for the passing years. I persevered and soon was lulled into the unreality of the puzzle of the mystery of two Christie murders, but I was in fact unable to summon the concentration required by reading. I kept coming back to Weena's Flowers. I wished there had been a copy of *The Time Machine* on the bookshelf.

I would know what to do? I would know what to *do*?

I soaked the Rose of Jericho and the Rose of Bethlehem in two glass dishes of water. In due course they both opened up, just as Trixie said they would. World War One and a desert scene came drifting into my mind's view. The white flowers lay, dry and ghostly, on the innocent oak desk in the Bass Strait Inn, far far, away from London, far from that bizarre future time of 802,701.

As I watched, the sun went down over the water, and the girl from the dining-room downstairs brought me some pinecones for the fire, and a hamburger with salad. Pot of tea. Two chocolates. I remembered how Trixie used to say chocolate flowed from the kitchen taps at her aunt's house. I had a bath in the bathroom down the hall. The water was deep and hot. But in truth the gentle water only reminded me that Trixie, once so warm and golden and chattering, had drowned in the swiftly flowing river, and now lay forever cold and white and silent in the forest, beneath the sheltering gum trees, among the little boulders marking the family graves.

I went to bed without finishing *Sad Cypress*. I didn't really care who had murdered anyone in fiction. I lay in the soft darkness of the old hotel in Burnie, the skies and the sea outside troubled by the realities of union strikes at the paper mill, clashes of the bosses and the workers. I was in a bewildering cloud of unreality as the eerie image of Weena's Flowers meandered across my consciousness. I told myself the whole thing was nonsense, just another one of Trixie's tall stories, a childish trick, a whimsical game—her own solution to the smallish problem of what to do with the three strange objects in the cardboard box. Those objects had become my problem. Toss them in the rubbish bin? Or send them back into childhood, back to where the fantasy began? Make Hepzibah smile as she remembers the lyrical lies of long ago? Did Trixie really give any thought to the matter of what I was going to do with the things? I believe she did. It is no small responsibility when the dead hand to the living such virtually worthless mementos of times past. What does one do with this ephemera? Are they in fact *worthless* memories?

I got out of bed and sat by the fire, placing a pinecone on the embers every now and then. I rang the desk and ordered a double malt. With it came another small supply of pinecones for the fire. I made some decisions. No, I would not contact Matthew Mean and enquire about the life and disappearance of great-uncle Phoenix. I would forget about all that, would let the whole nonsense of it fade right away. I would write and thank Matthew for the parcel. I would tell him about the Roses of Jericho and Bethlehem, but I would not mention Weena's Flowers. It would be as if they had never existed.

I put everything aside and went back to bed. And yes, my sleep was troubled. A storm blew up in the world outside the window, and I woke suddenly in the middle of a fierce dreamscape of rushing wind and leaping flames and flying boulders. The line from *Twelfth Night* whispered itself to me: *I am slain by a fair cruel maid.* I lay there, quite still for a long time, and gradually I understood there was no rational way to decide the fate of Weena's Flowers.

What I did was cruel and final. My mother used to say that you've got to be cruel to be kind. Is that true? I turned on the lamp, went over to the desk, picked up the Weena's Flowers and, with Trixie's letter, I dropped them one by one onto the dying embers of the fire. They curled in the heat and were reduced to smoke and ash. The letter flared up and died away. Then, in a quick bright moment of something like anger, I tossed the desiccated bones of the two roses into the grate. Those poignant little memories of wars burned slowly, and somehow sadly—and then died. A strange calm came over me. I left the forlorn silver bar from the Bethlehem rose among the embers.

FIVE

The next day I packed up early and went downstairs to check out. The sun was shining through the square glass panes of the door, casting bright spots on the grey-pink floral carpet. The girl at the desk handed me a bouquet of white tulips wrapped in sturdy green paper. There was a card from Matthew, thanking me for coming to the funeral, and wishing me a safe journey back to Hobart. They were those untidy tulips with frilly edges, reminding me ever so faintly yet distinctly of the petals I had burned in the grate. Yes, I destroyed Weena's Flowers. I will remember them forever. Yet as all the flowers from Trixie's mysterious parcel were reduced to ash, I felt a strange bright release.

O save me from the lion's mouth: for thou hast heard me from the horns of the unicorns.

YES MY DARLING DAUGHTER

In Australia, that big island surrounded by wild seas and glittering beaches, when girls go swimming in the ocean, they are sometimes eaten by sharks. Mothers hand over colourful towels and tubes of Ultra-Sheer, Dry-Touch 100 factor sunscreen, saying:

Yes, my darling daughter,
Smear this on your precious skin,
And don't go near the water.

Now, if you will, consider this:

Faraway in time, torrent and tempest, The Black Forest of Germany was affected by the last ice age, which resulted in the extinction of many species of native tree. This was in the Quaternary period of Pleistocene era, roughly or perhaps precisely between 2.58 million years ago and 0.012 years ago, that's if scientists are telling the truth, and they probably are. They have their ways of knowing. Back to the trees now—*Pinus sylvestris, Fagus sylvatica,* various *Quercus,* and *Ulmus glabra* have all survived, you will be pleased to hear, and they are all doing well. The Black Forest is located in the southwest of Germany, and is, as the name suggests, dense and dark to the point of being black. Sinister, you'd have to say.

Think of illustrations in old storybooks, coloured pictures of impenetrable layers of tall and sombre pine trees that will bewilder and even devour the traveller. The glowing redcaps of *Amanita muscaria* mushrooms peep up from the forest floor, scarlet, dotted with white. The artists and illustrators love them because they are so decorative, but Nature has coloured them Red for Danger because they can make you very ill and can even kill your dog. They are part of the sinister enchantment of the old folk tale forest. In some countries, including Australia, the law prohibits the cultivation and possession of redcaps. They contain several biologically active agents, at least one of which—muscimol—is psychoactive, causing hallucinations. Its cousins—the death cap and the destroying angel—really *will* kill you. You might sometimes find death caps and destroying angels included in fairy-tale illustrations but they are less vivid and appealing than redcaps. In picture books, the redcaps rule.

And there they are, redcaps, gorgeous and seductive, in the Black Forest, beside the winding path between the trees, the path that leads to the little wooden house with its singing scarlet roof and gleaming lattice windows. The doorknocker is carved from a block of *Pinus sylvestris* and is cunningly shaped to represent the head of a laughing goblin. Knock Knock. Who is there is just the Kapuze family, who are in fact today the focus of a great deal of media attention, as a result of the dramatic and tragic loss of their daughter Purpur. The fear is that Purpur, fifteen years old and strangely pretty and utterly charming, has been eaten by wolves.

You will have realised that within the big island of Australia, pretty girls of fifteen are not troubled by wolves. However, just beneath the glittering waves, in waters blue as the heavens and green a glass, there moves, in silent search of innocent prey, the shark. Yes, the shark in all his sleek and shimmering finery, in a skin fit to fashion the handbag of a Russian princess— the shark moves with fin and jaw and teeth towards the smooth pale thighs of that carefree girl in the bikini, the girl with the big striped beach towel. That girl, that one. Her name is Tracy, and she is more or less compelled to disregard her mother's wisdom. She will forget the goopy sunscreen, forget the warning of the waves, the words that beat with ominous dark shadows that torpedo just beneath the surface.

And look, there they go, the giggling girls, skipping round the ragged rocks, far far away from the trusty lifeguard, and the flutters of life-giving flags, and far from the music of the spheres on their headphones, and there they go, run run running as fast as they can, knees knocking, shimmering hair streaming. In they go, into the curling, curling waves, blue as the heavens, and splishetty splashetty, and oh my goodness—here comes the you-know-what, silent as a slither-snake, cleaving its swift and silver way, with rows of teeth as sharp as nanna's nifty needles and pins, as white as the chalk on the white cliffs of Dover. As white as toothpaste. Silent.

They found the towel and the sunscreen and the terry-towelling beach-robe. On the golden sand. No trace of Tracy was ever, ever found. They shot a few sharks. Maybe it was a strange man in a rusty four-wheel drive who said: 'Get in, Baby, this is your lucky day.' Maybe it was the Pied Piper in fluttering multi-coloured silks, leading Tracy up hill and down dale and into the strange country in the side of the hill. Playing on that pipe. Anyhow, they shot the sharks.

In the Black Forest, it's the wolves.

Now, once upon a time in Germany, wolves were extinct. They became a myth. A bit like that tiger in Tasmania. As of today (being 2019) the grey wolf went extinct in Germany about 150 years ago. But this century, this amazing twenty-first century, the wolves of Germany are back. 'Authorities' reckon there are about 1000 of them about the place. Putting aside the question of whether to protect them or hunt them down or whatever, there is the matter of the disappearance of Purpur Kapuze. On holiday from her convent school of the Holy Grave, Purpur, familiar as she was with the best way to deal with *Amanita muscaria*, set off one morning early with a basket and a little blunt knife. She was a lovely German stereotype with long shining blonde curls, rosy cheeks, sweet white teeth and long strong legs.

'Yes, my darling daughter (this was actually spoken in some German dialect), gather up the redcaps, but don't listen to any psychopaths along the way, whatever you do.' Did she say to watch out for wolves? Possibly. Was Purpur as disobedient as that doomed Australian Tracy? Probably. Carefree and footloose, possibly beguiled by some Frenchified wolf in French clothing. Fancy free.

Anyhow, the debate about what to do about the wolves certainly hotted up all over Germany.

They found the basket deep in the wood, and the mushrooms, real beauties, were spilling out of it, gleaming scarlet knobs, dotted with creamy white, spread across the mossy earth. No sign of a struggle. Not a drop of blood. Months later they found a silver holy medal tucked into the nest of a jackdaw. 'Oh yes,' said Purpur's mother, 'that's Purpur's medal. Her grandmother gave it to her when she was a baby.' But in fact the ownership of the medal has never been established beyond doubt. 'Oh, yes, it's hers, beyond a *shadow* of a doubt. You mark my words, it's Purpur's holy medal all right.' Forever after, the Kapuz family would light a candle in the window each night, in the hope Purpur would see it and come running in. So far, no luck. Her mother says she hears wolves howling in the deep dark heart of the thick Black Forest. She can too. Purpur's father says he can sometimes hear his daughter calling to him. 'Vati, Vati!' she cries, faintly on the night air as a marigold moon hangs sweetly in the branches of the *Fagus sylvatica*.

Readers are invited to form their own opinions as to what were the fates of Tracy and Purpur. Attached are some helpful quotations.

German proverb: All mushrooms are edible.
Some only once.

Another German proverb: Wolves will be wolves.

Plautus: Where there are sheep,
the wolves are never far away.

Rural Australian Wisdom:
Grow rich on a sheep's back,
unless it's a wolf in sheep's clothing.

Wisdom of the Australian Beaches:
Swim splishetty splashetty between the flags.

Carrillo Mean: It's not the ones you see;
it's the ones you don't see.

Wolf: Little Pig, Little Pig,
let me come in.

News From the Ice Age: The Black Forest was affected
by the last ice age, which resulted in the
extinction of many species of native tree.

Laughing Goblin: While there are girls,
there will be wolves and sharks.
You mark my words. Ha Ha.

FRENCH SAILOR GULLY

Extract from the journal of
Heinrich Muller
September 25, 1913.
Railway Hotel, Castlemaine, Victoria.

You may wonder why I am writing in my journal so far from my home in Vienna. This small rural Australian town is where I came in my latest search for my brother Franz who disappeared from the face of the earth in 1852. I have waited many years, perhaps a lifetime, to resolve this riddle. So here I am, at the age of sixty-one, talking to Larry Chan, a Chinese man who long ago sold picks and spades and tin dishes to the miners at a place called the Forest Creek. He took me out to French Sailor Gully, which was, he said, the place where a French miner drowned when the waters of the Forest

Creek invaded and inundated the claim where the French sailor was working. It happened swiftly, and the Frenchman could not be saved.

'Franz, his name was Franz. Nobody could understand him, and he was a sailor, so we just called him French Sailor. He was very young, and we never knew anything about him. After he drowned, we called the place French Sailor Gully. He had a big grey cat that ran away after his master died. We buried him here. Other men took his boots and his tools. He did not have any gold.'

The low bushes and rough spindly trees had covered all trace, as far as I could tell, of the events at French Sailor Gully, sixty-two years before. Nothing remains but the silence, and an eerie stillness. Was this the burial place of my brother Franz who disappeared a year before I was even born? I believe it was.

Franz was only seventeen when he left our home in Vienna one night in the spring. He was suffering from a broken heart and was never seen again. All my life he was mourned for dead. He had been madly in love with Louisa, the daughter of my father's darkest enemy. It was like the story of Romeo and Juliet, in some ways. A week before Franz disappeared, Louisa's family whisked her away to a convent somewhere in Germany.

I have heard the story, the legend, of the night before Franz disappeared so frequently that it is almost as if I had been there at the time. He was a powerful presence in the family, in the house, in my heart. All my life my mind has quietly hummed with little summaries: 'He ran away to sea. He ran off to find Louisa. He took one of the horses. He joined the army. He went to Paris. My cousin saw him on the beach in Rio de Janeiro. He fell in love with a dancer in Berlin. He entered a monastery, a remote monastery, in Belgium. He ran away to sea, and ended up, as sailors often do, seeking his fortune on the goldfields of California. Or perhaps even on the goldfields of Australia. Far, far away. He ran away to sea.'

The night before Franz disappeared, my mother, who was given to prophetic dreams and visions, had a presentiment of disaster. As she was slumbering beside my father in their high, deep featherbed, she awoke with a start. Was she dreaming, or did she really hear the ring of a horse's hooves on the cobbles of the courtyard below? She lay still for a long moment—in years to come she always said she could not forgive herself for this time lost—until she folded back the silky coverlet and crept to the window where she parted the curtains and peered out. Moonlight fell on the cobblestones of the empty courtyard. The heavens were striped with soft grey cloud. A faint breeze disturbed the line of poplars bordering the approach to the house. No horse, no human presence. A large grey cat, still as a statue, was sitting on the edge of the stone fountain as if contemplating some distant reality. Slowly the animal turned its head towards my mother. And what my mother saw, plainly in the moonlight, was that the face of the cat was the face of my brother Franz. He was smiling sadly. They seemed to stare at each other for a long, long time, spellbound, my mother said. And then before her very eyes the cat just disappeared. Faded. Dissolved. One minute it was there and the next minute it was gone, and the moonlight fell upon the cobbles and upon the fountain, and upon the empty, empty courtyard. The cat was never seen again.

She hesitated to awaken my father, but she lit a candle, and in her long white nightgown she tiptoed urgently along to the room where Franz would usually be sleeping. There, beside the bed, a candle was burning low. The bed had not been disturbed. And Franz was never seen again. My mother knew in her heart that something strange and even terrible had happened. She ran back to my father and they, together with our old servant Peter and also my three sisters, searched high and low. Nothing.

In the days that followed, in the weeks, the years that followed, they conducted an exhaustive search for my brother. I was born a year to the day after that dreadful night.

As for Louisa, she returned to Vienna after many years, residing in the Convent of Saint Elisabeth, until she died in 1912. And then it was that a nun at the convent asked me to call on her, for she had something of some significance to tell me. Thus I came to learn at least a part of the story of my brother's disappearance. For in the papers left by Louisa was a letter from Franz, sent from the distant goldfields of Australia in 1853. He gives the simplest details of his adventures, being intent upon assuring Louisa of his undying love. He will make his fortune, and he will return in triumph to claim her as his bride. He explains how he took a ship first of all to England from where he set out for New South Wales, working as a deckhand. The letter is full of youthful confidence and optimism. Finally, he made his way to the diggings at the Forest Creek, some seventy miles or so from the golden city of Melbourne. He was known by the other miners as 'French Sailor', for nobody understood him when he spoke.

Larry Chan and I stood in the forlorn and haunted gravesite at French Sailor Gully, a bronzewing pigeon moaning in the gum tree nearby, whooo, whooo, and I said a quiet prayer. From the earth I gathered up a handful of crumbling orange dust, mingled with the fragments of dead sticks and leaves. I dropped the little collection into the pocket of my coat.

'We never did know who French Sailor was,' he said. I told him: I believe he was my brother. I believe he was Franz.

ROUND AND ROUND
THE GARDEN

For thirty years now I have run an arborist and landscaping business. The name was invented by my daughter Clementine, when she was about five, and it grew on me. *Mr Lop-Lop.* You'd have to say it's memorable. Our real name is Brown, and when I'm not being Mr Lop-Lop I'm known as Capability. Actually, it's James Brown. But some of my work is more than capable if I do say so myself. The local Council often give me quite big projects.

My wife Madeleine and I have always loved gardens, but we have never really taken the time to make one of our own. She runs the giftshop alongside *Mr Lop-Lop*. Her business is *Round and Round*, specialising in garden ornaments and all sorts of teddy bears. She and her friend Nell used to make tartan jackets for the bears. The little ceramic ones are quite popular—people sometimes like to put them on graves. Clem works for both of us, doing the books and so forth. She always says Madeleine has a great sense of artistic design. She's probably right.

But you don't want to hear about all that. Down to business, yes?

The other day Clem said did I remember Gerry Godkin. How could I forget? But why was she asking. Well, she said, it seems his wife Lily has died, and he wants us to help re-organise the garden. In her memory? I said, and Clem said yes, something like that. Grief takes people in different ways—I've seen it. Before I called Gerry back, I checked the records to make sure I was dealing with the same Godkins. Same address. OK. I had sometimes wondered what became of the Godkins. Some clients you get to know. With others you just have to fill in the blanks.

This was the thing. Lily, a small pale nervous woman in her fifties, rang me about twenty-five years earlier and asked me to go round there and give her a quote. Scruffy trackies and a grey apron. Turned out she wanted the whole garden cleared. You will bring the stump-muncher, wont' you? She was particularly insistent about the stump-muncher. I told her that added a lot to the cost, but she was determined. There was even a kind of defiance in her mood. I don't want a single thing left in the ground, she said. So, I quoted, she agreed, the boys and I razed the block—mainly lots of mature native trees and shrubs set out in fairly random rows.

It took three full days to get everything done.

I can't wait till Gerry sees it, Lily said, rather slowly and with a kind of dreamy emphasis. He's away on Council business. It's a surprise. I asked if they would be needing any landscape design or so, but she said no that wasn't the idea. I kind of wondered what the idea was, but I didn't give it a lot of thought. She paid me upfront in cash. A bit unusual, Madeleine said, taking the words right out of my mouth as usual, and we went out for dinner at the Willy Wombat Grill. Madeleine was wearing a bright green scarf she'd just knitted. It didn't really suit her, but what would I know?

Two days later I was in the grotty local pub after work, and at the other end of the bar there was an old bloke drinking himself stupid. Not unusual. He was glued to the tv watching the races with a kind of glazed stare. But when a neighbour called out to me, he suddenly came to life. He jerked his head and stared at me for a bit, and then he staggered over, half a schooner in his fist. You Mr Lop-Lop? he said. I nodded. Then he held up his glass and slowly poured the beer over my head. Good job, Mr Stump-Muncher, he half-shouted, half-growled. People turned around then looked away. I wiped the beer out of my eyes, and two other blokes took the drunk by the elbows and hustled him out into the night.

That was Gerry Godkin, the barman said. His wife has left him. He's pretty cut up about it. Well, I could see that. Then the barman put two and two together and said to me—I guess you were involved in the thing with the garden, eh Lop-Lop? Gerry planted it all out when they bought the house. It meant a lot to him. More than she did, actually, we reckon. Well, they say she's gone to live with her sister, and he's by himself in the house with no trees. No children. People thought they were a devoted couple. Funny business. You wouldn't think it to look at him, but he works for the Council, got some kind of office in the Town Hall.

That was the last I heard of any of it for all these years. A few times I drove past the house. Early on the garden just sat there like a landscape on the moon with the neat weatherboard marooned in the middle and a Hill's Hoist always empty, as far as I could tell. It was one of those blank, sad houses with what Madeleine calls 'no personality'. For a long time, the place was just a wilderness—weeds everywhere. Then later the whole place was rank with weeds. Next somebody more or less cleaned it up and planted a whole regiment of hideous iceberg roses. Well, it was a fashion in those days. I can't stand them. And Madeleine is with me on that of course. I thought maybe somebody else was living there, but one time as I was driving past, I saw the woman—older, but with the trackies and the apron and so forth same as Lily's—making quite a good job of pruning the roses.

But as I say, the other day, Clem said Gerry Godkin, same phone, same address, wanted me to call him. Was he going to apologise for the baptism by beer? Not likely. Did I even want to speak to him? Guess what, curiosity got the better of me.

Gerry Godkin?

Speaking.

James Brown here.

Yes. Thank you for calling back. I have a job for you.

He gave me the same address from twenty-five years back and I went round. He met me at the gate wearing thick grey gardening gloves, a kind of wild triumphant look in his eyes. A thin stream of dark blood trickled down his cheek.

About half the rose bushes had been violently yanked out of the ground and were lying all over the place a bit like bodies on a battlefield. Not that I've seen a battlefield. Gerry waved his arms in a vigorous gesture, and I reckon those mad eyes were practically popping out of his head.

Now I want all this cleared. Really cleared. You can do it? I think you cleared this garden once, a few years ago, Mr Lop-Lop, he said.

I believe I did.

In the long look that followed, neither of us mentioned the beer.

Well, I would like you to give a repeat performance. As soon as possible. You will possibly need to bring your stump-muncher to deal with a couple of ancient tree stumps you seem to have missed last time. I will be away for a week. Just send the invoice when you're done.

When I got back to the office, I told Clem what had happened, and she said she had just read in the local paper that Lily Godkin's funeral was private and no flowers by request. It only took me a day to do the clearing. Actually, I hate working with rose bushes. They can fling themselves at any accidentally exposed bit of flesh and really dig their teeth in.

That would have been the end of it, except Madeleine's friend Nell of the tartan jackets died and we went to the burial in the new natural section of the old cemetery. Instead of headstones and stone slabs they bury you under a native tree, and the graves are heaped with stuff like twigs and feathers and toys and pebbles and photos and flags with poetry on them and so forth. You guessed it—as we wandered at random between the mounds under the straggly trees, we came to Lily Godkin's grave. And there, half-buried in the leaf litter was a framed photograph of the weatherboard house as it stood in a garden full of native trees and grasses. Stamped on the severe metal frame were the words 'In

Memory of Lily Godkin'. But the strange sad thing was this—resting on the ground beside the photo there was a small ceramic teddy bear with a faded blue satin ribbon round its neck. I sometimes think I will never understand people.

RECORDING ANGEL

'Angels have been, for millennia, in scriptures and myths, in hearts and minds, an expression of human aspiration, an inbuilt instinct to engage, not only with invisible worlds, but with invisible beings too, as a way of relieving anxiety about living, and about the inevitability of death.'

– Peter Stanford. *Angels, a Visible and Invisible History.*

'At the round earth's imagined corners blow
Your trumpets, angels.'

– John Donne. 'Holy Sonnet vii'

Dear You,

In seven vivid night visions, on seven vivid nights, I saw you, as on a glowing screen. You smiled gently, and you whispered to me.

'Tell me about the island. Tell me.'

And your tones were sweet and seductive. You were half concealed by the branches of an ancient willow tree, the Celtic tree of intuition, beside a quiet-flowing stream. For six times I put the strange request from my mind, from my heart. But on this, the seventh utterance, I made the decision to open for your interest some of the details of 'life' on the island of Nevermind.

I realise that not only are you, as I say, 'interested', but you seem to radiate a certain anxiety, as well as a disquiet. The plague that is sweeping your world exhibits to you in vivid detail the inevitability of death. I desire to comfort you, lady-vision, woman of the willow, with some fragments of the story of Nevermind.

To begin:

Having made contact with me, you possibly already know that I am Beau, Recording Angel. I was recently appointed to a permanent position as Island Archivist. It's a fairly lowly position here, in the scheme of things, but I am pleased and proud to serve. I am assigned what I consider to be the noble task of documenting the events and actions of everyone on the island of

Nevermind, throughout time, forever. That is, until the end of time, if that makes sense.

I once wrote a song in which I quoted that piece from the *Book of Revelation* 12:14 where it says 'for time and times and half a time'. Fantastic! The song I wrote using the line was quite a hit here on the island. Fortunately, the Bible has been out of copyright for aeons. I am fascinated by the idea of time, but I am not a philosopher, and do not propose to enter here into the myriad fine arguments on its nature or meaning. I have better things to do, oh yes.

You will recall that Gabriel is held to be the principal Recording Angel, once described as 'a man clothed with linen, with a writer's inkhorn by his side'. His work goes much, much wider than mine, which is restricted to what happens within the confines of Nevermind. My own inkhorn, filled with my favourite Montblanc Heritage Spider Grey writing fluid, is a most handsome Montblanc Starwalker. It is of course in my hand as I write, here at my desk, on the finest available writing paper designed to last until, yes, the end of time. As for what I am wearing—well, my suit is constructed from a fine creamy linen, grown and woven in Ireland by the house of Thomas Ferguson of Banbridge. I like to think it compliments my gleaming black skin. I have been described as one of the Celestial Narcissists, but don't let that worry you. It doesn't bother me, what people say. Naturally I order my suits from either Anderson and Sheppard or from Gieves and Hawkes. Savile Row. I sometimes think Anderson and Sheppard have perfected the art of fitting the jacket to accommodate the wings. My lovely shoes are usually either Benson Oxblood or patent leather Mayfair from Thomas Bird of London. My other favourites are my Urban Angel boots from Fluevog. I also have a nice pair of their black Eugenes. When I fill my pen in order to make my mark, I take care not to get any ink on my fingers, and particularly not on my suit.

As you can tell, dear willow woman, the Angels of my division are all particularly well-dressed. Fastidious.

You may be familiar with a painting by René Magritte, called 'Homesickness'. In that work, the painter has not only faithfully rendered the lion in the foreground but has actually done a pretty good likeness of me, but only from the back. And he has certainly not captured in any way the colour of my skin. My cousin Gerald the Herald has argued that it is meant to be him, but I know it is me. Gerald is so much shorter than I am and, I must point out, considerably less athletic. By the way, he favours the Gregory Peck '62 jacket from Huntsman. We have a very different style. I have never had any dealing with Huntsman, although the jacket in question has a certain je ne sais quoi, I will admit. That bold tweed can be rather mesmerising. And he owns a kaleidoscope of fruity bow ties. To give Gerald his due, he is one of the best trumpeters you will ever have the pleasure of hearing. I remember when he took up the instrument as a mere cherub, at about the age of three. He has never looked back. We angels are frequently accused of blowing our own trumpets, and you may find within this letter of mine, a certain truth in that statement. Once upon a time, Gerald used to love to tune in to the sounds at twilight in the Australian city of Melbourne. Apparently, there were little boys with raucous voices who darted about the place with bundles of newspapers crying: Herald! Her-ald!

Sometimes it's not easy to fit in all the things I want to tell you. I imagine you, as you sit beside the river in your soft pale apricot gown, reading these pages with, I hope and trust, some pleasure.

Going back to the matter of the ink in the Stargazer, my cousin Gerald told me a sad story about a recent king who splashed ink on his suit from a leaky pen when he was signing a condolence book after his mother died. Gerald, who spends a fair amount of time on Earth, for various reasons, sometimes adopts a strange vernacular, told me the king 'lost it'. I can confidently tell you my Starwalker would simply *never* leak.

You may be forgiven for wondering how it is that I am supplied with these lovely things. Well, all supplies to Nevermind are via the services of the Intra-Universal-Lacework. This very letter will come to you that way. Archangel Gabriel is in control of the IUL. I simply submit to him a Formal Request and wait a while and then, hey presto, a parcel from London or New York. I confess that my most frequent request is for packets of tea from Twinings. I am pleased to say I use a Moroccan silver teapot that used to belong to a French princess. Gabriel can get anything. Nothing is too much trouble. I love silver. The funds for all this come from The Fund, which is beyond my comprehension, but which is, I understand, inexhaustible.

I have sometimes been compared to the solid silver angel on the tip of the umbrella of Pope Sixtus the Fourth. Yes, I really have. Imagine that. Although I have often had occasion to visit Rome, I have never taken the time to check this information out. I wonder where I might discover that umbrella. I suppose it could be on display in the Vatican Museum. Oh, the things they show off in museums. Next time I am in Rome, perhaps.

It occurs to me that if you were to choose to leave your shady willow and travel by some means or other to Rome, we could possibly meet. Such things can be arranged.

There has long been a fashion, beloved by the Pre-Raphaelite painters in particular, to depict us as wearing a sort of sentimental renaissance woman's nightgown, sporting long and curling locks, yet we in this division have in reality always been, and will always be, perfectly and superbly masculine. What I have just said goes against a great deal of theological teaching on the *non-gendered* nature of the angel. And there are in fact divisions of female angels, but they are generally given a low profile in holy texts. The men, after all, write most of the texts. The prophet Zechariah, for instance, who records several human interactions with angels, notes that he observed two female angels carrying the thirty-six-litre vessel on their way to building some sort of shelter for the said vessel. There are quite a few female rogue angels, mostly found in the teachings of twentieth century spirituality, notably Muriel who wears a lot of flowers in her hair and is committed to the spreading of peace and harmony. We have in fact become the flexible receptacles for a vast range of ideas from 'aliens' in spaceships to cherubs on the handles of inexpensive teacups. For heaven's sake! Naturally, the human couples who are destined to meet and merge on Nevermind are selected from a full range of genders. And colours of course. Well, in a sense, those things don't really count.

Dear lady of the willow tree, all I know is what I know, and what I tell you is what I know. In one sense, I could say that everything I tell you about Nevermind is what might be called 'appearance'. Is this *reality*? What *is* reality? I suggest you take it all with a grain of salt and a little mustard. I am not a theologian myself, but in the event that you want to go more deeply into the finer ins and outs of things, I refer you to the works of Dante Alighieri and John Milton, and of course the Bible and the Qur'an. I might also refer you to a useful text, being *Angels—a Visible and Invisible History* by Peter Stanford. My cousin Gerald the Herald says it's excellent, as far as it goes. Personally, I have very little time to devote to reading or research.

Just one other story about the Archangel Gabriel. It is one I particularly like because it involves roses. And I am so fond of roses. Flowers generally, to tell the truth. When the Prophet Mohammed was away at war, he had reason to believe his wife Aisha was unfaithful. He asked advice from Gabriel. 'Observe what she has in her hand when she greets you upon your return from war,' said Gabriel, 'then instruct her to immerse that object in the waters of the pool.' The Prophet did as Gabriel suggested, and Aisha ran towards her husband, bearing a sheaf of ruby red roses from the garden. At Mohammed's request, she stretched out her hand and gently let the roses fall one by one into the pool. And as they met the water, they swiftly changed in colour until they all floated on the surface, a glowing golden saffron. This was a sign of Aisha's infidelity, and ever since then yellow roses have been a marker of the faithless lover. Better than a private detective, really.

As well as roses, for some reason I also like images of and stories about us angels and ladders—well there was Jacob's ladder of course, a fabulous thing. I seem to have drifted into a mode of telling you quite a lot about myself, don't I? Well, I am a Celestial Narcissist. About the ladders—one of my favourite sculptures on earth is that of the ladders of angels ascending the west front of Bath Abbey. You might get a chance to take a look. Of course, there are angels everywhere. It's a wide and complex field of study, and full of surprises to keep you busy. But before you get yourself carried away by, for instance, the *Book of Revelation*, bear with me, for I feel I should tell you a little more about myself.

You have obviously heard of me—my name is Beau and, in the past, I have worked off and on as a Guardian Angel. You won't find any mention of me in the Jewish, Islamic, or Christian lists of Angels, and I should warn you that in 2012 CE there was a Vatican ban on what are called 'rogue angels', of whom I am sometimes considered to be one. However, be that as it may, I have plenty of stories to relate.

My new job of Recorder is a small promotion. It's also quite demanding work. Although, since the fluctuating population here on the island never exceeds five hundred, you could be forgiven for imagining there is little enough to do. You would be wrong, for I must record the earthly lives from birth to death, and then I must follow closely, documenting as much as I can of the events and actions after death. I should, however, warn you that very little of note happens on the island where everything is devoted to the preservation of a kind of dreamlike bliss. The convolutions in the lives of the wards before their arrivals on the island are matters of considerable interest. I say 'wards' but maybe I should say 'inmates'?

Or even souls although 'souls' is such a mysterious and contested term. It's difficult, sometimes, with the vocabulary here. I think I'll stick with wards. That's what we usually call them. What brought X here, and why Y? Yes, lives on the island are generally composed of matters less complex and less interesting than lives before death.

Consider the Life Stories of Walter'n'Matilda

This tale will give you some insight into what brings people here, and how earthly time and place shift around like fragments of glass in a kaleidoscope to result in the relationships between our wards.

Walter died in 1878. Matilda died in 1867. On the island, where time is unmeasured, and where our wards retain the 'years' they had at their deaths, couples can form. Such couples may never have formed on Earth. Walter and Matilda each died at eighteen, which is in fact the youngest age for a ward to be accepted on Nevermind. There are no children here, and the sexual act, while being, I believe, beautiful in itself, can never here result in issue. 'Bodies' here are so very different from what you are accustomed to on Earth.

Walter lived and died in Australia. Matilda likewise lived and died, but in Austria. As you would know, the names of the two countries have sometimes been confused and conflated in common speech. He was the son of an Archdeacon in some kind of Protestant religion, she the daughter of a Catholic Archduke. Arch and Arch. You can see already there are little details here that would pique my interest, not least the matter of the religions.

I have opened a file called 'Walter'n'Matilda', and the first item therein consists of the lyrics of what is known as an 'Australian bush ballad'. For if you say 'Walter'n'Matilda' quickly and carelessly, you might be saying 'Waltzing Matilda', which is the title of the ballad. And indeed Walter, a boy with some musical education from rural Australia, swiftly picked up the rhythms of the Viennese waltz soon after arriving here on the island and finding his feet. He waltzed Matilda many a time in the sunshine and moonshine and starshine and shadow of Nevermind.

Not wishing to interrupt my narrative with explanations, I have placed further information on the relevant bush ballad in the General Notes at the end of the narrative. You will see there that the protagonist of the ballad becomes a ghost and haunts the place of his death. In a sense, my story of the wards on Nevermind is a type of ghost story. It's an unorthodox ghost story of course, but nevertheless, I believe, part of the ghostly genre. Beautiful but not scary.

Ghosts are one of the results of death, and the causes of death are degeneration, disease, accident, and, if you like, war. Also murder and suicide, both of which I count as a kind of accident. I think that covers it. I have an interest in all those things, although I will never personally experience any of them, being immortal. Of course, human beings often get a mixture of several methods. You might be an old person somehow involved in a war, accidentally bitten by a mosquito, consequently infected with a deadly disease. It happens. Oh, and starvation is another one—I just remembered that.

What kind of an angel am I, really? I tell you I am simply a sometime Guardian, and currently a Recorder. I am not one of the Seven Archangels known for their success as warriors. Think of Michael, for example.

How will death come to Walter'n'Matilda? Wait and see.

Among the Herald Angels stationed here, my cousin Gerald, a busy Harbinger, occasionally comes over to my office on his way to make various announcements in the refectory, and we discuss, among other things, the topic of the Manner of Death, something that is high on the agenda for conversations on the island. Destiny is another popular one, and it is something that occasionally occupies me and Gerald. We enjoy a cigar and a Drambuie and a talk after dinner.

When a new ward comes in and forms a couple, another couple that has been here for some of our unmeasured time simply disappears, dissolves in the

Waters of Nevermind. The population numbers hover between four hundred and ninety and five hundred. As for where they go after the Dissolution, I can't tell you because I don't know.

To be honest, I don't really know where Nevermind itself is located. My knowledge of many matters is limited. Before I was sent here, for instance, I had never even heard of the Island of Nevermind. The principal purpose of the place is to bring together people of the various genders who were originally intended, in the Great Scheme, to be couples in some way, but whose manifestation on Earth suffered, for whatever reason, some slippage, some glitch in time or place such that they never had the opportunity to meet. Stuff happens, things go awry.

If this were not the case, there wouldn't be any such thing as a story, would there.

There are sometimes couples here who once formed a couple on earth, split apart, roamed the earth on separate paths, even linked themselves to other people, then in the end, as it were, found themselves at one again on Nevermind. Human beings frequently imagine there must be one special ideal *other* somewhere on planet Earth. Must be—or must *have* been. I understand that in most cases there probably is/was. But that other is, quite often actually, never found during earthly life, and the originals of the couple never have the chance to form that couple. Sad. You will have heard of 'marriages made in Heaven', well Nevermind is a small and particular part of that important service. In the event that things don't work out even here, the unsatisfied single entities move on to another island, another level, the name and location of which are not known to me, except as Subsequent, which is the title of the file of names of single wards who have moved on. As you can see, matters are complex in the fabric of life after death. Extremely. Ultimately wards can look forward to the General Resurrection and the Last Judgement, the Last Trumpet, but there is much to be accomplished along the way. As the great Thomas Twining of Gloucestershire often used to say, 'There's many a slip twixt the cup and the lip.' You can tell that Thomas is one of my favourite characters in Earthly history. I regret the fact that he has never been sent to Nevermind. It would be such a pleasure to enjoy a regular cup of tea with him.

A little note here on 'time'. You can tell, can't you, Willow, that this is one of my preoccupations. Gerald and I are in fact writing a little opera called 'Up and Down Tempo'. We work on it 'after hours'.

I am writing this document in 2023 CE, yet the story I will tell of Walter'n'Matilda is mostly set during the eighteen hundreds. Not that this time-talk is particularly relevant on the island. Time and also place are concepts that don't really apply here. You will not find the island registered on any of your maps of the world. Physically, Nevermind bears some comparison to the island of Capri. However, wildlife here is purely imaginary, existing in the minds of the wards. Yet apparently present. If these ideas are bewildering, relax, Willow. None of this *matters*. But really you should see the birds and snakes and flowers they dream up! Creatures and plants that have died out on Earth appear to roam the pathways and bloom in the fields of the mind of Nevermind. They are dying out at a great rate on Earth these days, since human beings began to ramp up their reshaping of reality around the middle of the twentieth century CE. I am told there are fish in the sea around Nevermind, but I have seen no evidence. Many fewer fish in the earthly sea, I understand. Here there are trees and flowers to die for, if you'll excuse the expression. But nothing toxic. My favourites are the orange trees in big silver tubs, similar to those at the Palace of Versailles. Insects by the millions. Butterflies and bees are in. Mosquitoes, naturally, out. Some sort of balance, never yet achieved in the strictly earthly realm, has always prevailed on Nevermind. Weather, perfect, meaning it's whatever any individual ward considers to be perfect, within reason. No big storms. Some wards have received little falls of snow as a sort of gift. You can see the rules of life on Earth certainly do not apply. Well, that goes with the territory. No volcanoes.

I have already intimated that couples form here between people from different centuries. I could tell you about a medieval maiden who ended up with a failed astronaut. Or there's the sweet tale, another Austro-Australian one, about a twentieth century girl from Alice Springs who died in a boating accident when she was starring in a toothpaste advertisement. On Nevermind she met her destiny, a twenty-first century dentist from Vienna who was killed by a terrorist when he was visiting his tailor in Savile Row. No, relax, it was not at Anderson and Sheppard.

One of my favourite couples is that of fifteenth century Enea Piccolomini from Siena, and his beloved Elizabeth. They met in Strasbourg where the young Enea was on diplomatic business. They had a child who died, and Enea moved on to the court of the Emperor Frederick the Third in Vienna, leaving Elizabeth behind forever.

That was until they were united again on Nevermind. Oh, that was a glorious day. But before Enea showed up here, in the meantime he had had a varied and glittering career, ultimately being crowned Pope in 1458 CE. He was known as Pius the Second. But as you can see, the story achieved a happy resolution on the island. Nice name, Piccolomini, I always think. Have you ever read *The Commentaries*? It's his autobiography, and I believe it's the only such document ever written by a Pope. Imagine that! Do you like Tuscany? You can visit Enea's summer palace in Pienza, the Palazzo Piccolomini. I went there once. I know very little about 'Humanism', but I believe the Piccolomini was the first Humanist building ever made. Enea was ahead of his time, as they say.

But back to Walter 'n' Matilda for now. And for your interest I will also continue to document various details of the nature of the island itself, for as far as I know these things have never before been revealed to the English-speaking world. For instance, the language spoken here is not English. You may be reading this tale in English, Icelandic, palawa—anything really, since, whatever I write automatically translates for your convenience. The language spoken on the Island is that universal language spoken before the Great Flood, before the construction of the Tower of Babel, the place where the tongues divided. Walter spoke a form of English and some rudimentary French, and Matilda spoke French and German. However, when the wards arrive here, they are naturally automatically fluent in what I will term 'Pre-Babel'. In fact, they don't even realise their other tongues disappeared when their earthly hearts stopped their earthly beating. Earthly language, nationality, class, colour, religion—these are of no account here. Although on the issue of colour, I must say I have always been personally pleased with my gleaming ebony skin. Matters such as food, entertainment, housekeeping, and so forth are all provided by the Band of Angels, flown in as it were, when and where required. And there is always the IUL, as discussed. People sometimes wonder about sewage on the island. Well, all I can say is that yes there is a sewage system. And as for what might be termed 'rubbish', well that is daily dropped into chutes and sent off elsewhere, I know not where. Possibly to Earth, where there is a great interest, I understand, in the matter of rubbish and its disposal.

Now for the Romance of Walter'n'Matilda.

You can see that the time glitch between the death of Matilda and that of Walter was eleven years. Since there is no earthly sense of time here, Matilda's stay before the arrival of Walter would appear to have passed in an instant. As if time were manipulated in order to serve the higher purpose of correcting the original error whereby the couple were separated by circumstance. The best analogy I can offer you here is that of the dream. Everything here is somewhat similar to a dream. If that helps. Maybe it does, and maybe it doesn't.

The events that unfold within the dream state are outside time and place and human logic. So, it is on the island. Yes, think of the way it is in dreams—that's more or less the way it is on Nevermind. Although, even as I speak of ghosts and dreams, I am conscious the system here is so much more elegant than those things could ever be.

Matilda's apparent destiny within the royal circles of Europe was to marry Umberto of Savoy and become Queen of Italy. But as I know and you know poor old destiny was intending her for Walter, and hence the sad and drastic matter of her early death. Shocking really, the way destiny works sometimes.

Since Matilda died before Walter, I'll begin with her. She was the daughter of Hildegard who was the daughter of King Ludwig the First of Bavaria. This means that she was a first cousin of King Ludwig the Second who was the patron and lover of Richard Wagner, and therefore instrumental in bringing all that grand opera into being. Ludwig the Second was also known as the Swan King, and sometimes as Ludwig the Mad. I don't know much about all that.

Matilda was four years younger than her cousin, this Swan King, so you can imagine them as children sometimes playing together in the palaces and gardens of the Kingdom. Such imaginings are always rather sad in hindsight.

Something I really like about Matilda's father, Archduke Albert, is his nickname, Angel Heart. Well, I would like that, wouldn't I. He was known far and wide for his charity and generosity. Albert Angel Heart—it has a certain sweet ring to it.

However, as often happens, this kind old Angel Heart was a strict father, and you will see shortly how this strictness had apparently tragic results, results of great significance in the destines of Walter'n'Matilda.

The Viennese family spent the summers south of Vienna in Baden bei Wien, which is famous for its healing baths and generally pleasant atmosphere. But all has not always been rosy in Baden bei Wien. There is a startling reminder of when lovely Baden suffered from the plague, beginning in 1679 CE. This reminder is the elaborate plague column, erected in 1713 CE in thanksgiving for the end of pestilence. Always a cloud lurking somewhere, isn't there. Plague brings on a lot of ghosts. Several are recorded in the files on the island, wards whose destinies lay beyond death by plague. You will be able to sympathise with these ghosts, knowing, sadly, I am sure, ghosts of your own from the pestilence of 2020 CE.

It was Gerald who brought me the news of this particular pestilence. He said there might be quite a few new alliances forming here, alliances between recent victims and victims of earlier epidemics. There was the influenza after the Great War, and the Black Death that wiped out so many populations in distant centuries. He said he imagined Walter'n'Matilda might be moving on to make room for fresh couples. I will be sorry to see them go, but of course there is really no place here for nostalgia and sentiment.

Winters for Matilda's family were spent in Vienna where they enjoyed what is known as a whirl of social events such as ballets and operas and balls—you know the kind of thing. Diamonds and pearls and satins and silks and wines and roses etc. Music of course. Dancing. Romance.

There's that word. Romance! It's beautiful in its way, but dangerous. Red Flag.

Matilda was pretty and witty and popular, and I know of at least one young man who fell in love with her. This was the Archduke Ludwig Salvator who didn't have a hope of marrying her because, as I said, she was 'destined' to marry Umberto. Cue ominous music. This particular Ludwig never married at all, but he did have quite a few children. So that's something, I suppose. One of his girlfriends was Catalina Homar whom I mention because of my interest in disease. She went to Jerusalem, contracted leprosy, and died. I probably should research the files here to check whether Ludwig, and whoever might have been his destiny, passed through Nevermind. But the files are vast, and I really have to discipline myself and stick to the matter of Walter'n'Matilda. Ludwig, broken-hearted at the death of Matilda, went to the island of Majorca where he fell in love with the sea, the sky, the plants, the animals. This always seems to me to be a profoundly sensible and practical way to go on. I will prepare a short paragraph on him for the Notes, but suffice it to say here that on Majorca there is a glorious walk he designed, known as the Archduke's Path.

Now this is another dear little correspondence with the life of Walter, for in his Australian town of Castlemaine in the province of Victoria there is a walk initiated by and named for Walter's father. This is known as the Archdeacon's Path. The two Paths emphasise, in what I see as a *heartbreakingwarming* way, the immense class divide between Walter'n'Matilda.

There's the grandeur of one path as it winds across the rocky cliffs looking out to the Mediterranean Sea. (Those cliffs, that view, grand as they are, seem to me to be less magnificent than the cliffs and views of Nevermind.) There's the humble nature of the Archdeacon's path leading from Walter's father's charming little Australian sandstone church, down a short steep hillside, across a railway line, across a stream, and up a longer hillside to the old prison that sits on the top of the second hill, like a tiny medieval castle. Pause for a moment and imagine that Path.

The stream that is crossed by the Path moves slowly, choked here and there with rubble, seething and bubbling with malodorous refuse, portions of dead animals, and human waste. Think blowflies, think rats. Mosquitoes. And yes, think *disease*.

On a warm spring morning in 1865, the child Walter skips beside his father, Archdeacon Archibald Crawford, as they make their way down the rough gravelly path to that dank waterway as it gloops and eases through the valley. First, they will cross the steam railway line, a source of great wonder and fascination to both Walter and his father. Walter scrapes the ground with a stick, teases the rough grasses, pushes aside rounded stones that roll away into the low bushes. Eucalyptus trees stretch above the path, for a moment scenting the air with the blithe sweetness of their pale-yellow blossoms. Even their leaves are scented, I believe. Bright blue and red parrots squawk through the treetops, dart and flutter, waddle on the branches, swiftly sip up the insects hiding in those yellow blossoms. Tum-te-tum, Walter sings, and he swings his way, thrashes the trunk of a tree, disturbs a busy nest of ants. He is the image of a perfect little boy from the time of Queen Victoria, with his button boots, his belted navy-blue suit, his straw hat with a scarlet ribbon. He might be rolling a hoop through Hyde Park, sailing a toy yacht on the pond, watching a puppet show in Vienna.

This all sounds quite pretty, and it is. Apart from the quality of the stream and the small dark world of anguish and sorrow that is contained by those warm rosy-red walls of the prison up there on the hill. British soldiers in their stiff scarlet uniforms guard the entrance. God only knows what bestiality and squalor is going on inside the walls.

And furthermore, the scenery around here has been laid waste by the exuberant search for first of all gold nuggets, then alluvial gold, then quartz gold from underground. The feverish precious metal-focused invasion began in 1851, and lasted until the late 1860s. Leaving behind a ravaged, poisoned landscape of crumbling orange rock. Leaving many of the black people, who had lived on the land for millions of units of time, like lost bundles of burnt matches on a dead and dying fire.

So, when Walter and Archdeacon Archibald are going down and up the Path, the town of Castlemaine is a-throng and a-buzz around them with seekers after fortune busily raping the hillsides, chasing treasure, robbing each other, killing each other for gold. Two men in ragged clothing and wide greasy hats pass Walter and his father on the Path, heading for the fuss and hubbub at the centre of the town. Each man carries his possessions in a dusty bag on his back. Blanket, shovel, tin cup, tin can, knife, damper, rum. They tip their hats to the Archdeacon and mutter something in German. They are unsmiling inside their thick and rugged beards. Sunburnt faces.

If Walter were to scratch the earth where the grasses grow, he might lay his little hands upon a dusty lump of valuable glitter. It could fund his education far away in a place such as Oxford. Such dreams. The gold from around here will provide the funds for the kingdom of Britannia to finance its powerful and dominant self for the latter part of the nineteenth century. You should see the grandeur of the buildings in Great Britain, constructed on the wealth from Walter's little town.

Apparently, the Queen of England became so powerful she even ruled the waves!

Walter and his father are on their way to the red brick prison on the hill. Walter will wait outside the gate with the Redcoat soldier on duty. The Archdeacon will go through the small wooden door in the corner of the great wooden gate. The gate to a terrible castle. Be good, Walter, says his father. And the soldier winks, and Walter sits on one of the blocks of grey-gold sandstone beside the doorway, and is good. The child has a functioning Guardian Angel at this point, but as I know, and you know the contract will somehow break down by the time Walter is eighteen. These things are tricky. It's a strange thing, destiny.

When Matilda is about Walter's age, she is the perfect picture of the Austrian female child, a peaches and cream girl living in the highly civilised and privileged atmosphere of fancy musical Vienna. Velvet and satin and lace. Long brown-gold curls threaded with strings of roses on ribbons. She has singing toys and silver bracelets and a ring with a ruby, yes a ruby, in it. A little dog with a collar of Moroccan leather. Silken rosettes on her shoes. Could it be that the fine bright chain around her neck is fashioned from the rivers of gold that run beneath Walter's feet? Oh, she's a million miles from Walter's rancid waterway and brilliant parrots in the gum blossoms. And yet, and yet, if you put together the child-portraits of these two, they could, you know, be part of the same world. Just. Or almost. There is, I think, a refinement and a dazzling something about Matilda that is somehow at odds with the quieter blur of Walter's image. He seems to be still. She seems to be moving, shimmering with a confidence in the certainties of life. Is this just my fancy? Slivers of silver meaning slither through the forests of time. Perhaps it *is* all my fancy. Each child has beautiful, beautiful eyes. Oh, the sparkle! The eyes have it. And they are blue.

He played in the dust and grasses with sticks while she went to glittering parties and concerts and operas. And yet the eyes *do* have it.

The death of Matilda came, in fact, just two years after the day when Walter took his springtime walk with his father up to the red brick prison. But as I say, the time glitch is not important here, the key matter being the deaths and destinies that were going to bring Walter'n'Matilda together on Nevermind. The Romance.

There is one more filament of a link between the two. You may find this one to be too remote for your liking, but it amuses me, so I will tell you. Matilda's grandfather, King Ludwig the First of Bavaria, became besotted with the fabulous Irish dancer known as Lola Montez. She was King Ludwig's mistress for two tempestuous years, at the end of which the king abdicated and Lola left for Switzerland, never to return. The same Lola, after many more adventures, crossed the oceans and later performed her scandalous Spider Dance at the theatre in the distant little goldmining town of Castlemaine where the gold was financing Britannia. This was in 1856, three years before Walter's family arrived in the town, and four years before Walter was born. These things have their place in the records I keep on Nevermind, since time lapses are of course not relevant. Have I said that too many times? Or they are relevant in different and unusual ways. I merely point them out for the purposes of earthly narrative. If you look at it this way: Matilda's uncle's mistress visited the faraway spot, where Walter would first come into being, four years before the event of Walter's birth. Meaningless? Not the way we see things on Nevermind.

Now let's get to the events that gave rise to the Romance. By which I mean, the deaths of the protagonists.

Take Walter. Think back to the teeming thousands of gold-seekers. Think of the sizzling heat of the summers. Think of the waters of the creek, the rats, the flies, the fleas, the viruses, the bacteria. Overcrowding and poor hygiene. Yes, you guessed it—it's *disease*.

When Walter was eighteen, he contracted typhoid fever, which is caused by eating food or drinking water contaminated with the faeces of an infected person. Think of President Lincoln's little son Willie. Contamination can occur when food is prepared by a person who is carrying the disease yet is personally unaffected by it. Think of the famous Typhoid Mary who passed it to her hundred or so New York victims when she cooked their food, while never succumbing to the disease herself. She was an asymptomatic carrier of the pathogen. Her Guardian was a bright one, and no mistake. Those of her victims must have been lax. Incidentally, typhoid is not to be confused with typhus, which is transmitted by the bacteria contained in the bites of fleas. Typhus is mainly tropical. Typhoid fever happens just about anywhere filthy enough. The waters of the creek at Castlemaine were filthy enough.

Walter did not survive. No other member of the Archdeacon's household succumbed, and the true source of Walter's infection was never traced. In fact, the details of his demise were more or less suppressed, off the record. The Archdeacon did not wish for the people of his parish to realise this terrible illness had breached the very walls of the holy church. Walter lay in his small iron bed as the fever boiled and bruised his brain. Through the high window at the end of the bed squinted the bloody sinking sun, a scream across the pink sky behind the rosy castletop of the prison. Walter himself was covered with purplish-cerise blotches. He felt himself, part of himself—was it his heart—slowly lifting, painlessly lifting, fluttering and floating out to meet the sky-blaze of scarlet. Silent now. And Walter's heart sank with the sinking sun.

His friends, several young men, were inconsolable, and they put up a most elaborate, exuberant and glowing pair of memorial stained-glass windows in the south wall of the Archdeacon's church. Two long and vivid blazing panels show two images of Christ, one of the Resurrection, one of the Ascension. Above the panels is a small bright image of the Holy Ghost, the fluttering Dove. These faithful and sorrowful un-named friends were also responsible for the great stone slab and large cross that to this day lie flat on Walter's grave in the cemetery.

But Walter, as you know, moved on, and is now destined to live perhaps forever on Nevermind, with his true love, the vivacious Archduchess Matilda of Austria. Well, they will surely be here until at least the Dissolution. Until the end of time, perhaps. It's a thought.

Now for Matilda's story.

1867, and Matilda, having spurned the Archduke Ludwig who went on to become so very busy and important on the island of Majorca, is staying at the Vienna residence of the Empress Elisabeth. Wearing a glamorous new gown of shimmering cream silk, pale blue satin and filmy gauze, she glitters with diamonds and gleams with pearls. A fairy-tale Archduchess. Remember the bright blue eyes. She is about to leave for the theatre, is waiting by the window. On a small table to the side of her there is an ormolu and enamel box, all pink and gold, decorated as it happens with silly romping Viennese angels. It is filled with cigarettes. Although her father has forbidden her to do so, she lifts the lid and takes from the box a lovely little French cigarette. Thin and white and wicked. As she flicks it daintily, coquettishly in the air, a gallant young man holds out a lighted candle, and Matilda smiles as she draws air through the tobacco, and the tip of the cigarette glows red. She savours the taste, blows out the smoke in thin curling puffs. She has done this before. The young man smiles, turns away, and puts the candlestick back on the table.

Oh no, here comes Matilda's father, Angel Heart himself, striding towards the group at the window. If he sees her with the cigarette, he will simply forbid her to go to the theatre. Strict! Quick as a flash, Matilda conceals the cigarette behind her back. The large blue satin bow that fastens the sash of her gown is covered, misted, in a layer of palest gauze. When the gauze meets the cigarette, it instantly ignites, and the whole dress is suddenly aflame. Matilda's hair, pearl-studded, lights up. Matilda is a raging torch.

Two weeks of blinding blazing pain later, Matilda dies. The sight in her twinkling azure eyes fades as rushing flash-flash spinning stars dizzy and dance through the ringing hollow of her hairless skull. Matilda dies in an Austrian shroud, a weeping dislocation of duchesses and dukes shivering, hovering, lightly wafting. Like smoke. Matilda dies. Today her tomb is in the Imperial Crypt in Vienna. I have seen it. She moves on, ultimately to meet Walter here on the island. In no time at all, they are here, they are names and numbers in my Record.

Like all the wards on the island, Walter'n'Matilda inhabit small silken tents beneath ever-flowering trees, and they play and dance in the great glass auditorium known as the Crystal Palace. As I explained before, much that happens here resembles the quality of dream, drifting in and out of one pleasure or another with the ease of cinema. On the night the couple arrived on the island, before they went to their tent, they were celebrated in the Crystal Palace. And the Band played 'Waltzing Matilda'. Of course it did. Imagine!

Walter'n'Matilda are, I think, the sweetest most beguiling couple among the many-many couples I have observed and recorded. They seem to me to resemble each other in gesture and facial features. And when they waltz to the music of the great Viennese Johann Strauss, as interpreted by the Band of Angels, they resemble angels themselves, dancing on beams of celestial sunlight. I'm getting carried away here. But it's true. I see what I see, and I know what I know, and I speak as the Recording Angel of Nevermind. I note that Walter'n'Matilda are dancing, waltzing , into something like eternity.

So, there you are, Lady Willow. The story of the Island of Nevermind, and the tale of Walter'n'Matilda. I look forward to hearing from you with some details of your own life on Earth, and I imagine also that, one lovely day, one golden-glowing day, one starry-starry night, when you are called to rest, be it by disease or accident, or by the ravages of time, you may perhaps make your way on flying feet to the welcoming gardens of Nevermind.

I am your faithful servant. Remember that
Beau.

PS

I need to be careful to conceal this missive from Gerald. I am not permitted to spread all these stories around, and Gerald is quite literal in following the Letter of the Law. I fear he would report me if he knew I was doing this. And that would see me in all kinds of hot water. You will be discreet, won't you, My Dear Willow?

GENERAL NOTES

'And the Band Played Waltzing Matilda'

This is a song written by Eric Bogle in 1971. It tells a gruesome tale of the First World War, focusing on the tragic landing of the Australian soldiers at Gallipoli in Turkey in 1915. Quite a few of these soldiers have now passed through Nevermind, finding their sweethearts again.

Archdeacon's Path

This is a short winding pathway beaten by Archdeacon Archibald Crawford (1815–1890) from Christ Church on Agitation Hill in the Australian town of Castlemaine to the nineteenth century prison on top of the facing hill. Archdeacon Crawford was the Rector of Christ Church from 1859 until his death. Remember that the path crosses the murky stream that was probably the source of Walter's typhoid fever.

Archduke's Path

Archduke Ludwig Salvator of Austria (1847–1915), when blue-eyed Matilda rejected his proposal, built the path in 1883. Its mountain views along the northern coastline of Majorca gave him solace in his despair. The rambling pathway is eleven kilometres long, beginning in Valldemossa and ending at the snow house and the refuge of the Archduke's home, Son Moragues. Along the way you can see the remains of coal mines that were worked until the middle of the twentieth century. The cave of an anchorite named William, who died in 1635, is also on the way, which eventually leads back to Valldemossa. I did in fact check the files on Nevermind for this William the Hermit, but there was nothing.

Thomas Bird

The original factory was in Northamptonshire in the 1800s. These days the shoes (to die for) are made in Italy. Ah, that old Italian style!

Fluevog—Unique Shoes and Boots for Unique Souls

Motto: Good shoes leave small prints, no matter what your shoe size.

Yes, Fluevogs are eco-friendly. It all began in Vancouver in 1970. Ended up in New York. Then, of course, in the City of the Angels, as well as far and wide. Yay! First up, John Fluevog and Peter Fox started re-fashioning a whole lot of shoes from the early 1900s. These shoes had been discovered in a warehouse in Mexico. By 1980 Fluevog were making the Angel Soles. Angel Soles! Engraved upon them is the message: Resists alkali, water, acid, fatigue, and Satan. (I generally don't talk about Satan, but you can check him out online.) The idea for the Angel Soles was delivered to John Fluevog by an angel, in a dream. I don't know who that delivery boy was. Gerald thinks it was one of our other cousins, but I am not so sure. In any case, you can revel in the whole Fluevog saga online.

Gieves and Hawkes

Headquarters at Number One Savile Row! It got its two names in 1974 when there was a merger. The story goes back to 1771 and is a work in progress. They have notably dressed the British army, navy, explorers, royal family and so on. They dressed the Duke of Wellington. Times change, and these days they are owned by some people in Hong Kong. Stay tuned.

Maybe check out the website for pictures and juicy detail.

Huntsman

Henry Huntsman (great name!) founded his original bespoke tailoring business in Bond Street in 1849. The hunting and riding aristocracy of Europe flocked to him, and the shop is still immensely popular today. His very own breeches are on display in the window at 11 Savile Row. Again, check the website.

Montblanc Starwalker Extreme Ceramic Fountain Pen

The ceramic here is a high-tech material used in the car-racing industry to build braking systems.

Palawa

This is the language of the palawa, the First Peoples of lutruwita (Van Diemen's Land) which is an island situated to the south-east of the continent of The Great South Land or New Holland. The continent is currently known as Australia, and the southern island was, from 1856 until recently, known as Tasmania. Strange convolutions, I know, but the whole business of the island today is scarred by the way it was treated in centuries past. The British invaded the place in 1803, and occupied, and tragedy set in.

Pope Sixtus the Fourth (Francesco della Rovere)

Lived from 1414 to 1484; he was Pope from 1471 to 1484. He was responsible for the building of the Sistine Chapel. He also created the Vatican Archives. There's no need to get carried away with detail here, but he was apparently implicated in the Pazzi conspiracy whereby the Pazzi family tried and failed to displace the Medici and rule Florence. My main interest in him resides in the silver angel on the tip of his umbrella.

Prophet Zechariah

The *Book of Zechariah* 5:9-11 describes the women in angelic terms. 'The wind was in their wings; for they had wings like the wings of a stork.' Pretty marvellous!

Recording Angel

In the *Book of Ezekiel*, Chapter Nine, the Lord commands the man clothed with linen to set a mark upon the foreheads of those in the city that 'cry for all the abominations' that they might be spared from general slaughter. The man must, with his inkhorn, then record and report on the events in the city. This man was in fact the great Archangel Gabriel. He and many another recorder, myself now included, have ever since listed the names and the lives of all people across time, in various levels of detail.

The *Book of Revelation*, Chapter Twenty, is quite explicit and dramatic about the material that goes into the *Book of Life*, recorded by the angels, and opened on the Day of Judgement. 'Whosoever was not found written in the *Book of Life* was cast into the lake of fire.' Uncompromising! It's important to get your stuff into that particular book. The *Book of Life*. Everyone on the Island of Nevermind is in it, but as I say, my job is to go over their earthly actions, re-document them, and then add the events that follow on the island. For the record. I am giving you mainly the Christian references, but I need to point out the texts of other faiths besides that of the Christians more or less back up what I am telling you.

Rogue Angels

In 2002 the Vatican Congregation for Divine Worship published its *Directory of Public Piety* stating that all veneration and prayer directed towards angels must be exclusively focused on Archangels Michael, Raphael, and Gabriel. Any other angelic beings are classified in the document as 'rogue'. I see where the Congregation is coming from, since people often feel free to invent an angel, but all I can say is that those Archangels are going to be mighty busy if they are expected to do all the work. The publication also has a go at Guardians, a category that includes me, pointing out that *we do not exist*. I recall that in the eighth century Pope Zachary banned prayers to Uriel on the grounds of *his* non-existence. The things they say!

Thomas Twining

Thomas Twining (1675 - 1741) was fascinated by tea and time, and possibly by chance and accident. I am of course interested in all these matters. There's many a slip etc. Thomas is best remembered these days for his tea—English Breakfast, Earl Grey. He opened Britain's first tearoom at 216 The Strand, London in 1706, where it is still located. Being a smart businessman, he devised a logo which he registered, and which is the oldest registered logo in England. Maybe there are older ones elsewhere, but I wouldn't know. Three hundred years and more is a long time for a logo to be floating about on planet Earth. Thomas devised a family crest, but, Gerald the Herald tells me, he failed to register it with the College of Arms. Many a slip. Such matters are frequently the subject of the after-dinner chats between myself and Gerald. The crest can be described in a couple of ways. Gerald, who gets his Latin details from Stephen Michael Szabo, a Heraldry Consultant in Sydney, Australia, gives me the right and proper terms thus:

Arms: Sable a fesse embattled between in chief two mullets and in base a lion passant guardant Or

Crest: A dexter cubit arm grasping in the hand two snakes entwined round the arm all proper

Motto: Fortiter ac Fermiter

However, I will now describe the crest in my own words, proceeding from the bottom up. The motto translates as 'Strongly and Firmly'. Not really particularly inspiring. Next up there's a shield with a rather friendly lion waving at you in the base. Above the lion there's a bar of crenellations, and above that two five-pointed stars side by side. Above all that, emerging from a nice twist of leaves, there's an arm with a fist firmly holding two serpents whose heads point in opposite directions. Nasty and vigilant, those reptiles, I would say.

Now, going back to Thomas himself, and his interest in time. On an external wall of his house, Dial House in Twickenham, on a south-facing wall, there's a vertical sundial with the motto: 'Redeeming the Time.'

Oh, Thomas, I do like your spirit. And I do love your tea. I don't really comprehend what your motto means, but it rings bells, Thomas, it lights my fires.

Tower of Babel

A story in *The Book of Genesis*, Chapter Eleven, explains that Noah's descendants wandered to the plains of Babylonia where, having perfected techniques of brick building, they set about constructing a tower with the misguided aim of reaching Heaven. People can be so innocent. God interpreted this act as one of intolerable arrogance, and he confounded the project by splitting the common language into a great number of different tongues, and also by scattering the people responsible across the planet. Good One!

Waltzing Matilda

This song was written by poet Banjo Paterson in 1895 and was published as sheet music in 1903. It was first recorded in 1926 by Russell Callow and John Collinson. It tells of an incident in the life of a lone man who is wandering the roads looking for casual work. He stops beside a waterhole to boil up some tea, and along comes a sheep which he promptly catches, planning to kill it and eat it. But the owner of the sheep arrives with three policemen. They chase the man who jumps into the waterhole and drowns. That waterhole will be forever haunted by the ghost of the drowned man. Bummer!

There was a time when people wanted this song to be the national anthem of the country, but for some reason they chose instead something about calling a woman named Joyce on the telephone. Let us all ring Joyce, they sing in a rather solemn way. The language of *Waltzing Matilda* is Australian slang of the nineteenth century. Here is a little glossary:

Waltz: to travel on foot
Matilda: a kind of primitive backpack
Swagman: a lone traveller carrying a matilda, also known as a swag
Billabong: waterhole
Coolabah: a eucalypt of inland Australia, growing on the banks of intermittent streams
Jumbuck: sheep
Billy: metal can with a lid and a wire handle to attach it to the swag
Tucker: food
Squatter: landowner
Troopers: mounted police

The Lyrics

Once a jolly swagman camped by a billabong
Under the shade of a coolabah tree,
he sang as he watched and waited 'til his billy boiled
You'll come a-Waltzing Matilda, with me
Waltzing Matilda, Waltzing Matilda
You'll come a-Waltzing Matilda, with me
He sang as he watched and waited 'til his billy boiled,
you'll come a-Waltzing Matilda, with me

Down came a jumbuck to drink at the billabong,
Up jumped the swagman and grabbed him with glee,
he sang as he shoved that jumbuck in his tucker bag,
you'll come a-Waltzing Matilda with me
Waltzing Matilda, Waltzing Matilda
you'll come a-Waltzing Matilda, with me
he sang as he shoved that jumbuck in his tucker bag,
You'll come a-Waltzing Matilda, with me

Up rode the squatter, mounted on his thoroughbred,
Up rode the troopers, one, two, three,
With the jolly jumbuck you've got in your tucker bag?
You'll come a-Waltzing Matilda, with me.
Waltzing Matilda, Waltzing Matilda
You'll come a-Waltzing Matilda, with me
With the jolly jumbuck you've got in your tucker bag?

You'll come a-Waltzing Matilda,
you scoundrel, with me.

Up jumped the swagman
and sprang into the billabong,
You'll never catch me alive, said he,
And his ghost may be heard
as you pass by that billabong,
you'll come a-Waltzing Matilda, with me.
Waltzing Matilda, Waltzing Matilda
You'll come a-Waltzing Matilda, with me
his ghost may be heard
as you pass by that billabong,
You'll come a-Waltzing Matilda, with me.
Oh, you'll come a-Waltzing Matilda, with me.

Well, that's it for the Notes
O Radiant Woman of the Willow by the Stream
All this is now and forever
On the Record

REFLECTION

'Irony is just honesty with the volume cranked up'
– George Saunders

I have never seen a woodpecker. But it was first mentioned in my fiction in 1987 when I invented a small Tasmanian coastal town called Woodpecker Point. I included in the story a note on the 'legendary Tasmanian woodpecker'. Of course, there never was such an animal. There are no woodpeckers in Australia. This town surfaces again in 'Speed Bonnie Boat', one of the stories in *Love Letter to Lola*. I am fascinated by the naming of places on the planet. Names can change over time. Writing the word 'Tasmanian' in recent years feels awkward, since there is now a fairly general desire to return places in Australia to the names they had before explorers and invaders and colonisers claimed the lands and re-wrote the names. The official name of Tasmania nowadays is lutruwita. Hence, in 'Speed Bonnie Boat' the narrator refers to the island as lutruwita. Sometimes I say Tasmania, and sometimes I say lutruwita.

The stories in this, my eighth collection, frequently contain references, however slight, to earlier work, and there is a perpetual sub-terranean or sub-marine hum that sets up between and across my books. I have found my fiction overall to be a personal expression of my search for meaning in existence. There are many ways to go about such a search, but telling stories has always provided one of the clearest paths for human beings to follow.

Back in 1987 I invented a character with the surname of Mean. His first name is Carrillo, and it was he who wrote the note about the woodpecker. He flickers and flashes in and out of view across my work. He is a shape-shifting trickster, and he also provides the epigraphs for many of my books, dispensing his wisdom. He appears to have written many books himself, books with titles such as *The Mining of Meaning* and *The Meaning of Mining.* One of the epigraphs to this collection comes from his *The Moan of Doves in Moama*. He wrote that at a time in 2022 when many Eastern Australian rivers burst their banks, and towns were virtually destroyed by water. Moama is the name of a flooded town on the

Murray River, 'moama' being a word from one of the ancient languages of land. It means 'place of burial'. The story 'Speed Bonnie Boat' is a narrative Carrillo wrote, and comes from some mythical publication called *The Chronicles of Carrillo Mean*. He, of part Australian Indigenous descent, is one of the principal characters in my 1990 novel *The Bluebird Café*. He has his own Facebook page, but he doesn't post often. His daughter, Lovelygod, was the result of incest with his sister, Bedrock, and Lovelygod is central to the plot of *The Bluebird Café*, being an archetypal Australian child lost in the bush.

Like Carrillo, who emerged in his own way in his own time, the image of the woodpecker has occasionally swooped and pecked its way through my work. There is a forlorn pickled woodpecker in a bottle in my novel *Field of Poppies*.

The image of the bird is on the cover of one of my books on writing *Dear Writer Revisited*. It is also on my Facebook page. This one is the red-bellied woodpecker (*Melanerpes carolinus*) from the eastern states of America. I found the image in a small book *The Concise Encyclopedia of Birds* by Bertel Brunn, and to my delight the bird was shown flying in the centre of a wiggly red line. 'Undulation flight of red-bellied woodpecker' it said. This was gold. I am attracted to red string, red cotton, red ribbons, red stitching, and so I couldn't resist the picture. The red line bears a certain resemblance to handwriting, as well as suggesting a rather eccentric blood vessel. The red ribbon runs gloriously, wildly, through the pages of *The Cassowary's Quiz*, a picture book of mine, illustrated by Anita Mertzlin. The notion of a blood-red wavering line relentlessly and forever moving towards its unknown destination could describe a quality of my writing. I like to shift from the central issue for a while before swinging back to the point. And while there is no primary overall topic explored in *Love Letter to Lola*, there is a fairly consistent kind of slant on life in general, and a distinct recurrence of themes, motifs, and propositions. Between the extinction of the mournful macaw in the first story, and the touching belief of the angel that is faithfully recording the lives of the dead in the last, the narratives undulate along, peering at life and death from different angles, in varying moods. The threat of the death, the annihilation of the planet, broods, one way or another over this collection. But not necessarily in a conventional sci-fi way, although there is some sci-fi, some fantasy.

I was born at the beginning of the Second World War, and soon experienced the ever-present fear of an earthly nuclear holocaust that would wipe out everything. Of course, today the planet and all the life upon it are even more clearly endangered, one way and another. The consciousness of all this naturally informs my fiction. In the 'Animals' section of this collection there are six stories that address the question of the extinction of species. And three of the stories in 'Humans and Angels' are concerned with the end of time.

Stories generally deliver to a reader a particular writer's perspective on the complexities of being alive. They are the refinement and elaboration and articulation of the results of that writer's observation and curiosity. The focus may be vast, broad, or fine and narrow. Tragic or comic, peaceful or violent. There remains for the writer to discover the language, the tone, the mood, and the structure that will best express the ideas, and will best interest and engage and entertain and move a reader. It is a writer's job to do all those things. The ideal reader is the one who *gets it*. Which, I suppose, makes the ideal writer the one who gives it. Writers need to read a lot and to practice a lot of writing.

Yes, I sometimes indulge in these little homilies. I think it is in order to remind myself of what I think I am doing. I find it helps. In reflecting on the stories in *Love Letter to Lola*, where to begin?

Some of the stories here were written in response to invitations to contribute to journals or anthologies. I get a great deal of pleasure from responding to such requests, and without the requests the stories would probably not have existed. There is an urgency and intensity to the writing of short fiction, a response to a desire to fashion a narrative that can be read and savoured fairly swiftly. Somebody wants a piece of science fiction, crime, fairy tale, fantasy, romance, horror. The challenge is exciting and rewarding, and sometimes bewildering. Then suddenly inspiration strikes or dawns or whatever it does, and the story is on its way. Naturally, inspiration can come of its own accord, and I write a story just because I want to write it. There can be a long time between the inspiration and the execution. I was inspired at the age of eight to imagine writing about the suicide of a friend's mother, but it took me about forty years before I wrote the story 'Pomona Avenue'.

There are twelve stories about animals in *Love Letter to Lola*. Eleven of them are more or less recent, but one, **'The Affair at the Ritz'** was first published in 1996. I include it here because I think it was the first story I wrote from the point of view of an animal. The creature is a cockroach, and one woolly-headed reviewer, who didn't seem to have read it very carefully, assumed it was something I had nicked from Kafka. As if. No, Baa-Baa, I met the cockroach in the hotel bathroom, and I killed it.

Incidentally, a cockroach is possibly the creature most likely to survive a nuclear end-of-the-world event. But that's not the concern of the story. This one is a sad, distressed, grand-motherly storyteller, and was in fact written for performance, in the days when I was a member of the Melbourne Street-Poets. It was inspired by a real-life event, and is meant to be read in a wavering old voice, as the cockroach is dying. The cockroach has seen it all—human behaviour from beginning to end—love, betrayal, cruelty, kindness, folly. The lot. She is telling her final story, dying after having been attacked by a guest in a hotel, and speaking to an audience of spiders and insects. There is a certain kind of humour, but it is of the black, choking, creepy sort that can make a reader nervous, very nervous. Like several of the other animal stories, the cockroach knows the ways of humans only too well.

In 2018 George Saunders, one of my favourite writers, published *Fox 8*, a small book narrated by a fox. I eagerly got a copy, only to be disappointed by the fact the fox, while speaking English, has a poor grasp of spelling. I find this particularly irritating and, in a word, fake. It is in the form of a letter addressed to 'Deer Reeder'. After reading it I went quickly back to my story **'Fertile and Faithful'**, realising that the spelling and grammar in the opening letter from Aletheia are rendered in a flawed childish manner. Are the spelling and grammar too irritating? I decided to keep them like that, and I hope my judgement was good. Early in 2023, I read a letter a child had recently written to her grandmother, and I was pleased to see the spelling chimed with that of Aletheia. My letter from Aletheia is only a hundred and sixty words long, and I think it isn't too demanding. This story is one of the group in the collection that examines the matter of extinction, and the scientific hope of bringing back extinct species.

It is one of the stories written in response to an invitation to contribute to an anthology, *Futures,* which is a collection to be published in 2023 by Glimmer Press. In the story I take up a childhood pre-occupation with the thylacine. The last one known died in the Hobart Zoo in 1936. I have never seen the living animal. My parents had seen it in the zoo, and my father, who grew up in rural lutruwita, had seen them in the wild. When my grandfather was a boy there was a bounty on the head of the thylacine, so he and his friends used to shoot them and collect the money. You can't have wild tigers eating up the sheep. I have followed the creature's sad story, which came to me through these family anecdotes, up to the present, at which time scientists believe they are on the brink of bringing it back from the dead. Whether this is the right or wrong thing to do is not really an issue in the story. The thing is just a fact. Many of the stories in the collection are enriched by facts and embroidered with factoids, which I will discuss in relation to some of the other tales. I remember the first time I began to play with them, adding a little 'Reader's Guide' at the end of *The Bluebird Café*. Hilary McPhee, the publisher, found them a bit un-nerving, but agreed to include them. However, she added she hoped nobody else was going to expect to have such stuff in their novels.

My great aunt Jessie had in her possession a pincushion similar to the one in the story, and there is one in the collection of the Tasmanian Museum in Hobart. They are weird and alarming objects, a mixture of nineteenth century social refinement and ancient primitive animal savagery. I have responded to the various moods and atmospheres around the story of the animal. Excepting for the vocabulary of Aletheia's letter, I have used a biblical language and format. I have told the tale of the disappearance and reappearance of the thylacine, with a twist. The grief that lingers at the heart of the thylacine's saga informs my 'Fertile and Faithful', and throws an ironic and possibly ominous light on the 'final' paragraph. A reader from another planet could be forgiven for asking what on earth these human creatures think they are doing, first extinguishing their animals and then trying to re-create them.

Another resurrection story is that of **'The Comeback'**, which I wrote in response to an invitation to contribute to an anthology, *Thrill Me*, again for Glimmer Press, in 2021. With such a great title, a story could have gone anywhere. Crime, romance, fantasy—anywhere. 'The Comeback' plays with the thrilling and chilling idea of bringing back extinct animals. Like so many people, I have been watching the efforts scientists have been making on such projects for a long time. A fascination with extinction is a thread in my work, now lurking in the shadows, now surfacing, in its various forms. I see I make it sound as if my work might be a tapestry, and so it might. It's the wiggly red line at work.

The narrator of 'The Comeback' is the spirit of the dodo, so the language is unlike that used in 'Fertile and Faithful'. It speaks with some knowledge of the present day, while having a rich understanding of its own long history. This, and other stories here spoken by animals, is intended to arouse anxiety in the reader about the future of life on the planet. A particular sadness and nostalgia for the ruin of the past, a sense of possible coming doom, a faint glimmer of hope, an unease about the fallout of subsequent events. 'Stay tuned,' says the dodo, who rather likes to offer a few factoids, hoping that while you keep your ear on the right radio wave, your heartstrings might play the right note.

One of my treasured books is *Dodo from Extinction to Icon*, by Errol Fuller, and it is the source of much of my knowledge of the dodo. The book is rich in illustrations and contains masses of detail about the dodo I would have loved to work with. However, a short story can't get too encyclopedic, and this one is meant to be more or less conversational. The first time I ever heard of the bird was when I read Lewis Carroll as a child. I had to learn all of *Alice* by heart for elocution classes, and the Dodo spoke in a deep, sad, lugubrious voice. If I were ever to read my story aloud, I might have to adopt that voice, but I think it would probably be unbearable in such a long monologue. On the other hand, I also think the voice would be appropriate to the slow deep sadness of the whole saga. I should say that the works of Lewis Carroll have had an effect on my own writing, as have many of the works of other writers I read long ago, such as Charles Dickens and Richmal Crompton. The idea of bringing animals back from extinction didn't come into my consciousness until much later. I just used to accept as given the idea the thylacine and the dodo were lost and gone. However, these days many people, including myself, while feeling a nostalgia for the past, have also a weird, sad, haunting 'nostalgia' for the future. There is a sense of powerlessness that is not always comforted by the various optimisms of scientists. It is that weird feeling I am addressing, really, in the animal stories in the collection.

As is often the case, I think, with writing fiction, I didn't realise I was exploring that feeling that until I had done it. Over the past few years, since I have been working on such stories, science has been reporting progress on the cases of my animals, and I have realised these stories will one day be just part of the history of all my own dodos. On a fancy little silver plate, I am handing to my playful critics a useful little note saying: 'Dead as a Dodo'. The word 'dodo', by the way, is an English word from the Portuguese 'doudo' which means fool. I suppose a fiction writer is a bit of a fool. It's possible the bird was so named in the seventeenth century because it seemed to be innocently willing to befriend the sailors who only wanted to kill it and eat it. Innocence and purity are synonyms. The innocent and the pure put themselves in the way of the knowing and corrupt. Good and evil, again. The stuff of life, the natural plasticene of fiction.

'**Resurrecting Martha**' is another tale of a bird species wiped out by the careless rapacious greed of human beings, and then finding itself on the laboratory list. This time it happened more quickly, the gap between extinction and promised resurrection being short and recent. The passenger pigeon was declared extinct in 1914 and is now on the rocky road to recovery. My story was published in 2022 in *Phase Change*, in response to an invitation from Twelfth Planet Press, the title and the name of the press being clues to the speculative nature of things. The last words of the first sentence of editor, Matthew Chrulew's 'Introduction' to the anthology are: 'catastrophic climate changes'.

'Resurrecting Martha' focuses on the clear human agency in the disappearance of the pigeon as being the principal factor in the rush to the total breakdown of the planet's systems. It moves from science to art, conflating the two ways of looking at things so that each seems to be as useful or as inept as the other, the tiny details of each being so trivial in the face of the grandeur with which they are tinkering. There is a little injection of religion with the presence of the Virgin Mary. The throwaway 'hasta la vista' at the end is a kind of helpless, useless attempt at hope.

Martha doesn't narrate this one. It is told in a rather nasty impersonal third person fairy tale tone, with notes at the end clarifying who all the key characters supposedly were. Is science the answer, or art, or religion, or is it all just fantasy? The dislocations of earth and of life on earth are here writ small. The final note is the final irony.

The first inspiration for the story came from *The New Yorker*. I have a habit—quite a few actually, but this one will do for now—a habit of reading the *New Yorker* every week, finding interesting articles, not reading them, tearing them out, tossing them in a big box, and leaving them there, piling up. Then sometimes I go to the box to find something to read. One day during the pandemic lockdown I discovered a story called 'The Birds' by Jonathan Rosen from January 6th, 2014. The subheading did it for me: 'Why the passenger pigeon became extinct'. It's a long review of a book *A Feathered River Across the Sky* by Joel Greenberg. I bought the book, and it took me to Joel Greenberg's blog www.birdzilla.com. Before I knew it I was writing 'Resurrecting Martha'. I think the big *New Yorker* box is a good habit.

I recalled from childhood the rows and rows of cages full of racing pigeons that stood in a field at the top of 'the back lane'. This lane behind our house was a rough track running uphill from the local bakery, up past the back fences of a row of houses on the left—on the right going past a little apple orchard, past some cowsheds, past an open sloping field where golden gorse bloomed in the summer. It was a dangerously uneven track where children, myself included, raced billy-carts. Once a boy and I stole some apples from the orchard and were chased off by an angry man with a gun. And eternally cooing in their cages at the top of the hill were the pigeons.

Writing the pigeon story, fiction, opened the way to memories of life in the back lane—visiting the strange man who milked the cows, obediently singing 'It's a long, long way to Tipperary' to encourage the cows to give more milk. Sometimes a memory gives rise to a story; sometimes a story stirs a memory. The pigeons in the back lane are nowhere in the story, yet in my heart they inform it. I remember fondly the boy whose father owned the birds, and then I remember he is now dead. My life and my fiction really are interwoven. It seems to me that the only way I can explain my work (and to a degree to explain my life) is to present the two responses to things woven *together*, somehow. And so, I construct a piece of fiction. 'Resurrecting Martha' is a long way from the back lane and the cowshed. Or is it?

In 2003, a friend asked me which book I would like for Christmas, expecting me to name a novel. She was surprised when I said *Spix's Macaw* by Tony Juniper, which turned out to be a most moving and informative account of a bird life-story that is almost surreal in its detail. After reading the book I was inspired to write **'Love Letter to Lola'**, another story of extinction. The history of the lost macaw is very moving, and has captured a wide interest, becoming the material for the movie *Rio*. Because the whole thing was so heartbreaking, I wrote the story as a love letter, in over-the-top vocabulary (but with perfect spelling). As it was first published in 2018 in *Australian Short Stories No66*, it ended with the sign-off from the macaw, but in 2022 came the news that the macaw was close to resurrection. I added a note from a cousin bird who has read the letter. I gave the title of the story to the title of the collection, sort of imagining the whole book as a letter to readers.

A great deal of the blame for the extinction of the macaw lies with collectors who treasure the birds and remove them from the wild to lock them up in cages. In **'The Cockatoo's Question'** the narrator has a swipe at people who keep exotic birds in cages. This narrator is a sulphur-crested cockatoo, and the stories it tells are in fact straight from the life of my village. The only invention here is the idea that the wise observant bird is talking to you. The anthropomorphism of these animal stories seems to me to resemble, in a way, the innocent anthropomorphism of a children's story, while laying open the follies of human behaviours. The tale was written during the summer bushfires and was published in *The Age*. It is a fairly straight cry for change in human behaviour as the changes in the planet itself become more obvious and uncontrollable, as the earth races towards its own extinction. I think cockatoos always look old and wise and sardonic, and I hope Caca is all of those things.

When Notre Dame Cathedral was on fire in 2019, I was moved to write **'Surveillance'**. This is another narrative from a creature, like Caca, this time a blowfly, carefully observing human lives. It was sickening yet mesmerising to be sitting at home in comfort watching the graceful old cathedral billowing with black smoke and orange flame. The Paris police resembled swarms of blowflies or cockroaches in their gleaming black uniforms and alarming Perspex masks. Set in a Paris church, this story leans towards religious detail, pondering life and death from within a frame of history and saints and angels and the arts. Some factoids again. The tragic death by fire of the ballerina Emma Livry has always fascinated me, and in fact it is part of the narrative of my first novel *Cherry Ripe*. Like the blowfly, I have never been able to bring myself to go to the museum to contemplate the fragments of the costume the dancer was wearing when she caught fire.

However, I have not had any problem looking in awe at the treasures from the tomb of Tutankhamun, as referenced in **'It's Mosquito Thing'**. This story is told by another vector of pathogens, this one being more casual and chirpy than the blowfly. I wrote it in 2022 when the floods were just starting and the news began prophesying a tsunami of disease-bearing mosquitoes. The floods and the insects, and the diseases, are of course motifs in the burgeoning narrative of the ominous changes in the climate of the earth. Hearing about the coming swarms, I remembered some detail of the role of the mosquito in history. One famous one I decided to leave out of the story was the one that bit Rupert Brooke somewhere in a foreign field that is forever England. It seemed a pity to leave him out, as his story is rich and fascinating, possibly too rich and fascinating for one mosquito to ease into the tale of Tutankhamun. That's something that often doesn't get mentioned when people talk about writing fiction— there are nearly always elements the writer must decide to leave by the wayside. Perhaps they will linger, and will come back some other time. But there is always just *so much* to write about. Life, so complex. Time, so long. Death and insects, so ever-present. Then there are the spiders.

When Queen Elizabeth's coffin was, beneath its Royal Standard, being paraded before the enormous throngs in the streets of London, the television cameras were having the time of their lives. Reporters would interview a weeping woman who would reassure everyone she had loved the Queen since they were both children in the Blitz. Then the camera would zoom in on the coffin, showing in detail the rather wild bouquet next to the orb and the sceptre and the crown. Sometimes, I, the watcher on a sofa far far away, would glimpse, on the white surface of a card that nestled among the flowers, what appeared to be a green spider. I sent a photo of the card with its little visitor to a friend, Lynne Kelly, who is an expert on spiders. She said that it *might* be a green orb-weaver. Jackpot! The royal orb and the orb spider. That was enough for me. Margaret Orb-Weaver had been born into fiction. Forget the interviews with the weeping woman, it was time to interview Margaret to discover her role in the solemn, colourful, grand, expensive, and lengthy ceremonies of royal death and burial.

'Margaret Orb-Weaver—The Interview' is delivered in the regular voice of a television interviewer and that of a frank and honest member of the public who is eager to give information, and delighted to be having a moment in the spotlight. Margaret is a spider on a sacred suicide mission, but I was pleased to see she could be just a little critical of the fact so many black bears had to die in order to provide the busbies on the heads of the Grenadier guards. These days my eye is more or less always on the wild and weird things humans do to undermine the safety of the planet.

The rat in **'Completing the 1080 Project'** is another creature preparing for its own death. While Margaret's death is linked to that of the Queen as part of service to the monarchy, the rat has made his own private decision to die in his own way. He is very resourceful, knowing his best poison, and researching his material online. In the course of researching the past of his own family in a kind of flurry of narratives before he dies, he garners details of science, history, religion, art. Rats first appeared in my fiction when I published a suite of rat stories in a collection called *The Common Rat*. Carrillo Mean provided the epigraph: 'Rats, they're only human.' Well now the rat has spoken with his human voice. The story was written during the pandemic lockdown, and I was obviously influenced by thoughts of plague. He warns his audience that the rats are taking charge, and he looks forward to the time when the planet 'boils over'.

From the rat who knows well the streets of New York, to the dog, Woffie, who lives on the streets of Melbourne. One day when I visited my dentist in his rooms above Dolce & Gabbana in 'the Paris end' of Collins Street, I passed a sleeping woman on the pavement. I had often seen her there, homeless, unconscious, tucked up under a blanket and surrounded by neat bags of possessions. I think she had a little white dog. I mentioned her to the dentist, and he told me how he had tried to offer her free dental care, but the police had told him not to do that. 'Who takes care of these people?' said the dentist, sadly. And the words 'who takes care' set off a memory of a song on one of my father's old 78 gramophone records: 'Who Takes Care of the Caretaker's Daughter?' Somehow, in the way these things happen, the story **'The Caretaker's Daughter's Dog'** came into being.

Then the animal stories take a complete leap from musings on the mad melancholy of everyday real-life into the realm of fantasy. I think the fantasy is even sadder. Here is the promise of the eternal nothingness of at least two species that never existed. **'The Tale of the Last Unicorn'**. The unicorn speaks in the manner of the storyteller in Rudyard Kipling's *Just So Stories*, addressing the reader as 'Best Beloved'. The ideal reader, remember, the one who *gets it*. I have a beloved and slightly battered 1953 copy of the *Just So Stories* given to me a long time ago by one of my writing students.

From the nowhere-nothing of eternity, the unicorn reflects on the way the world has gone from beginning to end. His companion is the Rainbow Serpent from the origin story of the first inhabitants of the land that is now Australia. The unicorn mingles her story with his own medieval European tales in which his mythical species was cruelly hunted down. Prints of the five pictures of the 'Lady with Unicorn' from the Cluny Museum hang in my study, a window into medieval Europe, here in the goldfields of Victoria, on ancient Dja Dja Wurrung land. I particularly loved writing this story.

So much for the stories told by the animals. To sum up in abstract terms the business of whether the story is told by a cockroach or a unicorn: The agency of the narrator's point of view governs the purpose of the narrative.

Moving from the animals now, to the humans and angels. One of my all-time favourite reads are fairy tales. They are often presented by a simple, authoritative storyteller. Third person, past tense, once upon a time. Job done. It always amazes me that the moral of the story of 'Red Riding Hood', a tale that has been told over and over for ever and ever has not yet sunk into general consciousness. Girls still insist on putting themselves in danger's way. I realise there is the argument that this is not the fault of the girls. Victim-blaming is useless after the event. But I tend to think that safety precautions are useful, generally. And it seems to me it is still clearly risky for attractive young girls to wander alone in the woods—or in the empty streets at night—or—well you name your dangerous places of choice. You can't really expect the wicked wolf to ignore what seems to be the opportunity of an innocent invitation. Then there are such things as Tik Tok that are not unlike the woods that led to grandma's house. When the editors of the *South of the Sun*, a modern fairy tale anthology, asked for a story, my heart was full of the tragic death of a young Melbourne woman called Eurydice Dixon. As she walked home from work through a park one warm night in 2018, she was murdered by a stalker. My story **'Yes My Darling Daughter'** is a very nasty brittle fairy tale response to that murder, told by a rather relentless storyteller. Carrillo Mean has his say at the end, but the last word goes to a cynical laughing goblin. I must say that it is a terribly, terribly sad little exploration of the links between life and fairy tale.

The title of **'Round and Round the Garden'** brings an old nursery rhyme into the fabric of lives in an ordinary Australian setting. It is narrated by a fairly ordinary man, James Brown, who is telling tales of love and grief. I have combined two unrelated stories from real-life. They happened many years apart, to different people, but the second one reminded me of the first, and hence the story James Brown relates. Flowers are a frequent motif in my fiction, and the sad roses in the story lead me now to the flowers in **'Two Thirds of the Truth',** which was written in response to an invitation to contribute to the anthology reflecting on *The Time Machine* by H.G. Wells. It is back in the home country of the Mean family, this time focusing on their flower farm. This takes me back to the novel I wrote when I was thirteen. It was the story of a family who had a flower farm and who lived in an apartment above a flower shop. This work has not survived, but I hear its echoes in 'Two Thirds of the Truth'.

The first flowers I ever cultivated, when I was six, were tulips, scarlet with golden throats. I had a flowerbed underneath a nectarine tree.

The narrator of 'Two Thirds of the Truth' is a Jewish woman who has lost a lot of family in the Holocaust, and now her dear childhood friend, Trixie Mean has drowned. That's quite a good name for a Mean, Trixie. The narrator says she thought, when Trixie the storyteller or 'liar' told her tales, that she could hear an angel speaking. Could this be throwing forward to the angel who tells the story in 'Recording Angel'? There's also a unicorn, not to mention the pincushions made from the jawbones of thylacines, as found in 'Fertile and Faithful'.

I didn't really notice all these threads until I began reflecting on 'Two Thirds of the Truth'. Do they matter, one way or another? Probably not. I happen to own a Rose of Jericho and a Rose of Bethlehem which do in life what Trixie says they do. Then there's a glancing reference to the ghastly history of the lost head of William Lanne, a story of gross colonial savagery that surfaced in *The Bluebird Café*.

A strange little thing happened. When the editor of the anthology first read my story, he realised he had forgotten about the existence of Weena's Flowers in

The Time Machine. This fact seemed to chime quite nicely with my story. The same editor had invited me to write a story for an earlier anthology *War of the Worlds: Battleground Australia*, again focusing on H.G. Wells. This one is '**Speed Bonnie Boat**'. Both anthologies are published by Clan Destine Press.

Unlike Hepizibah in 'Two Thirds of the Truth', narrator Carrillo reads *War of the Worlds* in the course of the story. Carrillo puts his spin on the history of lutruwita, drawing parallels between the British invasion of the island, and the Martian invasion of England. In fact, H.G. Wells said the attempted genocide of the Indigenous peoples of lutruwita was part of his inspiration for writing *The War of the Worlds*. So, it didn't take long for me to decide that my story for the anthology was about the delayed Martian invasion of lutruwita in 2019. I loved writing from the point of view of Carrillo. Usually, I just write his quotes for epigraphs, but here was a chance to give him wings.

'**French Sailor Gully**', for an anthology, *Goldfields*, flips right back into nineteenth century Australia, when gold was found and lives were lost and people disappeared forever. I often look at the ruined red rocks of the landscape around where I live in Castlemaine, and I almost believe I can see and hear the ghosts. Whenever I go to the hairdresser, I park my car beside a burnt sienna wall of raw rock that is pitted and ravaged from the work of the long-lost miners. Above the rocks grow scrawny gumtrees, grey and blue and greenish white, that stretch sigh, skeletons beneath an unforgiving azure heaven. There are many such places around here. The bronzewing pigeon in the story was moaning in the gum tree at the end of my drive as I was writing. It is also the source of the doves in the epigraph by Carrillo Mean. Not far from where I live is the one of the very saddest little graveyards I can imagine. It is called Pennyweight Flat Cemetery and is the resting place for babies and children who died of hunger and disease during the years of the nineteenth century gold rush. There are very few visible headstones, and those are mostly illegible, emerging from rocks and weeds, shaded by a few starving gum trees. The lost miner in the story doesn't even rest in such a place, but the story itself gives his brother a certain resolution and a forlorn sense of closure. The melancholy of the landscape around me in Castlemaine is present in this story.

The final tale, **'Recording Angel'** was inspired by a true story of nineteenth century Castlemaine. There's a particular pair of stained-glass windows in the Anglican church that fascinates me. I decided to look into their history, and so 'Recording Angel' came into being. This story also explores life in Castlemaine in the nineteenth century. The narrator is the angel Beau who narrates my novel *Red Shoes*. In the novel he was a Guardian Angel, but now he is the Recording Angel on a particular island reserved for certain people after death. He is handsome and fashion-conscious and has beautiful gleaming black skin. I imagine him as resembling one of the tall slender young Sudanese refugees who live in Castlemaine. A convenient tiny link emerged between the church windows and the life of an Austrian archduchess, Matilda. Consider the words 'archdeacon's path' and 'archduke's path'. The story of Matilda's death is similar to the death of Emma Livry, who appears in both 'Surveillance' and *Cherry Ripe*. Beau sets out to tell the love story of Walter and Matilda, and in the process, he takes pleasure in describing life on the island, and his duties there. He is another character who delights in bringing in the factoids.

When I was a child, my family would tell tales of a flood that inundated Launceston in 1929. I saw the high-water marks just below the ceiling of a pharmacy in the low-lying suburb of Invermay. The family's main interest in the flood was the fact that my mother's brother, Geoffrey, died from typhoid fever. Geoffrey was a kind of family saint, a myth, a sorrow. He was also a symbol of lost beauty and lost possibility. He was a term for heartbreak. So, I have always been interested in typhoid fever. I have a habit (another one), when I read a novel, of making a note of any mention of typhoid fever. Also mentions of teeth, actually. It turned out that real-life Walter died in the same way as Geoffrey, the filthy creek running through Castlemaine being a breeding ground for the disease. Thus are the elements of fiction woven deep into the fabric of life.

So runs and runs the wandering red line, stitching and looping its narrow sinuous probing path through my fiction, perhaps showing the way in an endless search for meaning.

WORKS PREVIOUSLY PUBLISHED

'Love Letter to Lola', *Australian Short Stories* 66, 2018.

'Margaret Orb-Weaver, the Interview', *Meanjin Online*, October, 2022.

'Resurrecting Martha', *Phase Change,* Twelfth Planet Press, 2022.

'The Comeback', *Thrill Me,* Glimmer Press, 2021.

'Fertile and Faithful', *Futures,* Glimmer Press, 2023.

'It's a Mosquito Thing', unpublished.

'Surveillance', *Saturday Paper*, 2022.

'The Affair at the Ritz', *Automatic Teller,* Vintage, 1996.

'Completing the 1080 Project', *Saturday Paper,* 2022.

'The Cockatoo's Question', *The Age*, 15 February, 2019.

'The Caretaker's Daughter's Dog', *Meanjin* Vol 78 No 4, 2019.

'The Tale of the Last Unicorn', *Island Magazine,* 151, 2017.

'Speed Bonnie Boat', *War of the Worlds: Battleground Australia,* Clan Destine Press, 2019.

'Two Thirds of the Truth', *The Time Machine,* Clan Destine Press, 2023.

'Yes My Darling Daughter', *South of the Sun,* Serenity Press, 2021.

'French Sailor Gully', *Goldfields,* Accidental Publishing, 2018.

'Round and Round the Garden', *Verge Magazine,* 2023,

'Recording Angel', unpublished.

ABOUT THE AUTHOR

Carmel Bird won the Patrick White Award for Literature in 2016. She has published novels, short stories, and non-fiction. Her 2022 memoir, *Telltale*, foregrounds her Tasmanian origins, as well as her lifelong interest in the natural world, and in reading and writing. *The Stolen Children – Their Stories*, which she published in 1998, is an early landmark work in the promotion of indigenous issues. *Love Letter to Lola* is the latest offering of an author who is known for the sharpness and originality of her narratives.

ACKNOWLEDGEMENTS

I wish to express my gratitude to publisher Bronwyn Mehan, editor Camilla Cripps, and cover designer Bettina Kaiser for their skill, generosity, enthusiasm, and support throughout the production of *Love Letter To Lola*. Also, I thank the editors of journals, newspapers, and anthologies in which many of the stories have been previously published.